# Ten Mi͟ ͟ ͟ ͟s

A Collection of Stories and Poems by
Hove Library Writers

Copyright © 2012 Hove Library Writers

The moral right of the author has been asserted.

Apart from any fair dealing for the purposes of research or private study, or criticism or review, as permitted under the Copyright, Designs and Patents Act 1988, this publication may only be reproduced, stored or transmitted, in any form or by any means, with the prior permission in writing of the publishers, or in the case of reprographic reproduction in accordance with the terms of licences issued by the Copyright Licensing Agency. Enquiries concerning reproduction outside those terms should be sent to the publishers.

Matador
9 Priory Business Park,
Wistow Road, Kibworth Beauchamp,
Leicestershire. LE8 0RX
Tel: (+44) 116 279 2299
Fax: (+44) 116 279 2277
Email: books@troubador.co.uk
Web: www.troubador.co.uk/matador

ISBN 978 1780881 423

British Library Cataloguing in Publication Data.
A catalogue record for this book is available from the British Library.

Typeset in 11pt Aldine401 BT Roman by Troubador Publishing Ltd, Leicester, UK

**Matador** is an imprint of Troubador Publishing Ltd

Printed and bound in the UK by TJ International, Padstow, Cornwall

# Contents

| | |
|---|---|
| Introduction | vii |
| | |
| Anne-Marie Norman | |
| Virginia | 1 |
| The Story of Jane | 13 |
| | |
| Bob Glaberson | |
| Bernie and Me | 18 |
| Henry in School and Out | 21 |
| Manna from Heaven | 23 |
| So this is it | 25 |
| | |
| Deborah Waldon | |
| Christmas at Auntie Delphie's | 27 |
| Funny Turn | 33 |
| I Killed My Grandad | 38 |
| The Last Will and Testament | 44 |
| Reunion | 47 |

## Helen Bedford

| | |
|---|---:|
| Check the Tides | 50 |
| Little Silver Hat | 52 |
| Soul Mates | 53 |
| We Meet Again | 55 |
| Winter Snow | 67 |

## Jenufa Harris

| | |
|---|---:|
| What Would I Do to Protect the One I Love? | 68 |
| The Tartan Blanket | 71 |

## Karen Antoni

| | |
|---|---:|
| Electricity | 75 |
| Half-Listening | 80 |

## Kay Beer

| | |
|---|---:|
| Marriage Proposal | 83 |
| Rainbows End | 84 |
| Kissing the Pavement | 91 |
| Poisonous Thoughts | 101 |
| Left versus Right | 108 |

## Liv Singh

| | |
|---|---:|
| A Master of the Universe | 116 |
| After the Revolution | 119 |
| No Fixed Abode | 122 |
| In the Secretary's Words | 123 |
| The Yard | 128 |

*Contents*

Rob Manley
Larkin Poem 137
From 'The Long Good Morning' 140
BFI 143
The Wonderful World of Slate 149

Solera Russell
Fading 152
Grandmother's Cottage 163
Robot Romance 166
The Library 170
Alien Encounter 173

Ziggi Rock
A Stranger in a Strange Land 178
St. Finan's Bay 180
Stillness 182
The Lost Beloved 184
Beastly Presents 186

Author Biographies 189

# Introduction

In the autumn of 2007 New Writing South sent out a few flyers and posters advertising a new writing group at Hove Library. As a pilot for a new 'writers in libraries' scheme, Hove one was of three such groups set up with Brighton and Hove Libraries.

On the morning of the first meeting New Writing South facilitator Kay Sexton arrived at the library to be overwhelmed by what she faced. Not only by more than 50 writers trying to fit in a room that accommodated half that number but also by an anxious librarian concerned about the health and safety issues of such numbers.

Almost four years later and the two groups established that morning: Comedy of Errors and The Hatchery are still meeting every month and both are vibrant and strong. From those early beginnings participants have increased their skills, boosted their confidence and developed their own writing. One result is this fine anthology of work from eleven authors drawn from both groups, including many of those founding members who were determined to squeeze in to that small room all those years ago.

New Writing South is proud to have played a role in the support and development of both Comedy of Errors and The Hatchery. Since their formation a further six library writing groups have been established in which all kinds of writers informally meet, receive support and take advantage of development opportunities offered by New Writing South.

None of this would have been possible of course without the support of our partners at Brighton and Hove Libraries, not least all the staff at Hove who continue to host and welcome the writers.

Acknowledgement and praise must also be given to Kay Beer and Liv Singh whose commitment, hard work and inspiration has got this anthology into print and into your hands.

Chris Taylor
Director, New Writing South

# Virginia

Anne-Marie Norman

Susan Moggeridge called out for Virginia as soon as she got home. She would scuttle from room to room and, if it was summer, from house to garden until she had located her companion. The thought of coming home to find Virginia injured or gone was too upsetting to bear. She hung her mackintosh on the peg by the door of the cottage. It had been a demanding day. Councillor Gambling had needed humouring after a lengthy Council meeting about overcrowded graveyards. The local journalists had gone away with the idea that body snatching would soon be rife in Lewes and it was going to be reported in tomorrow's newspaper. Gambling had resorted to a string of wisecracks beginning with a pun about having a "coronery" heart attack and ending with one about digging himself a hole. It had been left to Susan to laugh at all of them. 'I'm taken for granted, I really am', she had told the office. But in the administration of the Coroner's records for the Town of Lewes she was meticulous and indeed was quite an expert when it came to death. It had been she, when the weather had been unusually hot one summer and several of the white freezer trucks that picked up dead bodies had malfunctioned, who had come up with the idea of employing a small army of ice cream vans to take their place. It was also Susan who had noticed when her colleague, Harriet Dolphin on the neighbouring pod, had died, when everyone else in the office had thought she was merely asleep after a hectic morning of pre-away day meetings. Susan had put a cosmetic mirror in front of Harriet's mouth to see if she was breathing and had then raised the alarm when no mist had formed. She had received plaudits from three managers, one senior, for her efforts. These she had printed out and stuck to her fridge with magnets.

It was nearly autumn in Rodmell. But though the temperature had dropped the sun in certain parts of the garden was still strong. Virginia was outside on the lounger, in one of those sunspots, with a smile on her face. Not all cats had her expressiveness, her elegance, her long, sleek hair and dark green eyes which were only half open most of the time. But they opened suddenly the moment she heard the handle go down on the kitchen door.

'Oh, my darling there you are,' cried Mrs Moggeridge. She moved assertively for a short woman, almost marching across the lawn on her stout legs. 'Have you been sunbathing?'

The cat responded by stretching its entire body in an arc and then relaxing again. Mrs Moggeridge stood on tiptoe to glance over the fence, then folded her skirt under her and sat down next to Virginia. 'Have you missed me?' The cat yawned, then stared at her as if she were a necessary

*Virginia*

inconvenience. 'Yes you have. We've missed each other, haven't we?'

Up the road half a mile, though Susan was unaware of it, a car had run out of petrol. The driver had seen the sign for the village a little too late, then had been forced to turn round in a field, almost skidding into a ditch. It was lucky the car had stopped just as he had reached the village pub and he had managed, with the help of a local patron, to roll it onto the paved area near the porch.

When Phillip had caught his breath he walked in through the low front door, stooping as he did so, and almost bumping into a hanging basket of flowers. 'Do you have any vacancies?' he asked the landlady. 'Car's died.'

'No, dear, we're full up at the moment,' she replied. But she gave him a napkin with the address of a local bed and breakfast written on it in black biro. Number five, it said, and there was a map next to it with two parallel lines, five squares and a dot. He hadn't expected such friendliness. In London no one wanted to talk to you, let alone call you "dear".

Phillip walked down the lane trying to see the numbers on the cottages but the gardens were long and the walls high. Every house seemed to have a thatched roof and all looked immaculate enough to be boarding houses of one kind or another. He was in awe of the flowers overflowing from the bricked gardens though he wasn't sure of their names. Honeysuckle came to mind. But the smell...the smell was like perfume or better; better than anything you could buy over the counter in Harrods or Harvey Nichols. He had the idea of counting the houses and when he had come to the fifth one along he walked through an archway created by an evergreen bush, continued up a winding path and knocked on a wooden door. A short woman with blue button eyes answered.

'I'm looking for a place to stay,' said Phillip.

'Oh, are you lost?'

'Yes. Well, the woman at the…Scottish name… Abergavenny Arms, said you might be able to put me up.'

Mrs Moggeridge let out a little laugh. 'Did she? Silly girl!' She looked him up and down. He was smooth-skinned and smelt of a dry, woody aftershave. He was wearing black-rimmed glasses and carried a leather briefcase. All of these things pointed to refinement and civility.

'My name's Phillip.'

'Susan.'

'I seem to have run out of petrol. There's no garage. I had a conference today, you see, then, when I was driving back…I'm never any good with maps.'

Mrs Moggeridge giggled. 'Of course,' she said, 'come in. You can sleep in my husband's room.'

'Won't your husband need it?'

'I doubt it.'

'How much do you charge?'

'Charge?'

'How much will it be for the room?'

'Oh dear!' She giggled again.

'You're not a landlady?'

'No, no! Goodness, no!'

'Oh, I am sorry. I think I've made a mistake. I was supposed to go to number five,' he said prodding the napkin.

'That's Fleur. She's all full at the moment. Students, rats, roaches and ants. She's only got two rooms and they're very small. But you're welcome to stay here with me.' Phillip supposed these country villages were all full of people who had retired and were desperate for company. He'd have to pay her something but now he was tired and it was easy to accept the invitation.

Inside the cottage it was light and spacious. He had assumed it would be dark and small. There was a chintz sofa and behind it a grandfather clock that told the correct time. He was led into the kitchen where at once he noticed two enormous china bowls on the floor, one brimming with water, the other containing what looked like finely chopped steak.

'I see you have a dog.'

'A cat. She is a bit on the large side but I don't mention it within her hearing. I have to buy everything for her from the dogs' range at the pet shop.' She pulled out a chair and gestured to Phillip to sit down, then bustled around him with teapots and cups.

At that moment the door opened and the subject of the conversation entered, appearing quite unsurprised at the visitor's presence. She jumped gracefully onto the Welsh dresser and seated herself between two ornamental blue plates so that she was above both humans and looking down at them. She tilted her head upwards and sniffed at Phillip, then stared at him intensely, as if she wanted an explanation for something; something he was guilty of but had forgotten.

'I think my poor little angel's hungry. She's shy because you're here but usually when she wants something she gets up on her hind legs and she puts her little paws up just like this.' Mrs Moggeridge raised her arms to her chest and did an impression of a cat that made her look more like a squirrel. Phillip responded with a polite smile. Old bag's been living alone for too long, he thought. I suppose she thinks I'm her new best friend. Then something red and still caught his eye on the mat underneath the cat flap.

'Oh, I think it's got a mouse.'

Mrs Moggeridge leaned towards the door. 'Oh dear, we don't want any mice.' She pulled out a drawer, put on a pair of rubber gloves quite clinically, bent down and picked up the punctured carcass between thumb and forefinger. 'Out, out, out!' she cried, and the offending thing was whisked away into the evening and disposed of in an outside dustbin.

The cat regarded the performance with an air of amusement then turned its attention back to the visitor.

'It's got very long hair,' said Phillip. 'I suppose you have to brush it every day.'

'Oh yes, it takes hours. We don't like the comb, do we darling? Only the brush.'

'What's its name?'

'Virginia Woolf.'

'Like the author?'

'Exactly. We get a lot of tourists here, even at this time of the year, mostly Americans, because of the Woolf connection.'

'Connection?'

'Yes, she used to live at the house across the lane.'

'I didn't realise. How interesting.'

'She died here too. It's a sad, sad thing when someone so talented wants to do that to themselves.'

'Oh, yes, she...drowned, didn't she?'

Mrs Moggeridge wrinkled her nose.

'Wasn't there a film about it?'

'Yes. We do get a lot of people just coming to see the river. Have you read her?'

'Not much. I think she's a bit overrated frankly. Yes, a bit slow. Not enough action for me. Still, I suppose that sort of thing always entertains a small percentage of the population.' The cat, who had been licking an upturned paw, stopped abruptly and fixed him with an unwavering stare. If Phillip hadn't known better he would have called it malicious.

'Virginia, of course, has her own room. Mine is at the top of the stairs and yours will be on the left. View of the garden. Perfect now but we did have a few problems with the fence. The man who lived there before never used to mend it so we complained. Not a good response.'

'Won't your husband mind me staying?'

'Goodness, no. He only visits occasionally. He's in a home: Seagull's Heaven. It's just down the A27. Sometimes his batteries run out, you see. Bowel problems! He needs irrigating and I just can't bring myself to do it. Anyway, as I was saying, our neighbour, nasty man, got quite militant. He took it out on Virginia. Of course everyone in the village was on my side. He was a bird man. He thought Virginia was trying to get at his budgerigar. She wasn't, of course, she was only having her little game. She plays little games, you see. She runs after them like this.' And Mrs Moggeridge did an almost balletic impression of Virginia running and swiping the air with a paw. 'Anyway, one day she came back in quite a state, soaking wet and crying. She wouldn't leave my side for days.'

'What happened?'

'Who knows? Who knows what that cruel man did? Anyway, we have a new neighbour now: Crispin, he restores stained glass windows. We get on very well indeed.'

'What happened to Mr…?'

'Dunnock? He moved away.'

Mrs Moggeridge opened the fridge door to get some milk for the tea and Phillip couldn't help noticing that it was full of meat, mostly poultry, which looked as if it had been freshly caught as it was still feathered. The old woman continued to busy herself around the kitchen and then suddenly, with no warning at all, did a little pirouette and slid behind her guest. He felt a light pull at the back of his neck and tightened his shoulders. A cold finger slipped inside his shirt and down his back, causing him to shudder and jerk his body round instinctively. The woman withdrew her hand swiftly. 'Your label was sticking out,' she said, 'I have a thing about labels. They have to be tucked in.' She breathed in sharply and sighed.

Phillip fingered his neck. 'I'll do it myself next time.'

Mrs Moggeridge pursed her lips tightly. 'Oh dear, did I scare you?' she said. 'I'm watching you, you know, I'm behind you.' And her giggle was like a half-formed hiccup. 'Just a joke… just a joke.'

Phillip attempted a casual smile but his mouth twitched at the corners and gave him away. He was aware that his heart was beating slightly faster than it had been. I won't have to put up with her for much longer, he thought. I'll go to the pub and by the time I get back she'll be in bed with her Ovaltine.

*Virginia*

'I think I'll go for a walk,' he said, 'see the river, get a bit of exercise.'

'Shall we both go?'

'No! I...don't want to put you to any trouble.'

Mrs Moggeridge frowned. 'It doesn't look like it did in the film, you know. Very bare and no weeping willows. It's twenty minutes down the lane. I'll leave the key under the flowerpot.'

Phillip walked out of the cottage, back through the hedge and down the lane. He passed the house of Virginia and Leonard Woolf. The gate was firmly locked but he could see a garden with a wrought iron chair in it shaded by an elm tree. He shivered, unable to forget the sensation of cold fingers against his neck. He was not used to such intimacy with people he had only just met and he had a vague feeling that the old woman had done it just so she could touch his skin.

After twenty minutes he was still walking and there was no sign of a river. The fields were marshy and uneven. He had already slipped into a clump of nettles and was becoming irritable. He bent down to scratch an ankle and when he looked up he could see that he was alone except for a few sheep and an abandoned tractor. Twenty minutes along the path, Mrs Moggeridge had said. He checked his watch. There was a chalk hill in the distance and a windmill but he couldn't see or hear a river. He continued to walk, not wanting to give up. Perhaps the "river" was one of the streams on either side of him. But they were too dry and shallow. You couldn't throw yourself into one of those and expect to drown, even if you had put rocks in your pockets.

Then all of a sudden he came to a bare promontory. He climbed it quickly, expecting to be disappointed, but there, revealed at last, was the river. It was wide and deep and powerful and the wind had created a stripe along its back. It surged forward as if its mission was to engulf anything in its path that resisted. Phillip sat down on the bank, carefully avoiding the white rocks and stones around him. And then the strangest thoughts filled his mind. He wondered what had happened to the neighbour who had assaulted the beloved cat. Had he really left the village, or just disappeared? Perhaps he had visited this very spot. Perhaps he had fallen in accidentally…or been pushed. He'd have been dragged under by that tide in no time at all. Phillip put a hand behind his head protectively. He looked back at the path. Mrs Moggeridge could have been there, she could have crept up, put her hands around his neck and… But why was he imagining such ridiculous things? She was just a lonely old woman. He got up and hurried back in the direction of the village.

Reluctant to return to the cottage while his hostess was still awake, Phillip decided on a tour. He wanted to feel he'd made the most of the country experience. He passed an old army bunker and a church and saw more shades of green than he had in a long time. Of course as it was a small place it wasn't long before he found himself back at the Abergavenny Arms; it seemed to be the hub of the village and therefore a natural place to linger. There was a comfortable leather sofa which made it hard to leave so he ordered four large gin and tonics, one after the other, and downed them swiftly. By the time last orders were called he was feeling mildly disorientated and rediscovered the cottage only by recognising the weather vane sticking up from the roof.

'I'll sleep on the sofa,' he said to himself. 'I'll leave as soon as it's light and avoid the old bag altogether.' He ran his fingers down the wall in the hallway but was unable to locate a light switch so he staggered blindly into the kitchen, throwing a half-eaten packet of crisps and some Alka Seltzer onto the table.

Suddenly he heard a deep gurgling sound close by. It was quite rhythmical and was getting faster. He looked around the kitchen still trying to focus through the gin and half darkness. Then his eyes found the source of the strange, churning noise. Just between the vegetable rack and the back door was the cat. It was crouching down very low on the tiles, lurching forwards at intervals, retching.

At that moment Mrs Moggeridge rushed into the kitchen.

'What have you done?' she demanded, glaring at Phillip.

'Nothing,' he replied, slurring his words, 'I've only just got back.'

She turned on the kitchen light and ran to the cat.

'Look at her. She's in agony!'

'I've only just seen her,' said Phillip, quite dazed by the light.

'You've been drinking!'

'I was going to help. It was throwing up when I got here.'

The enraged woman's pink face turned grey, she turned and looked at the pills on the table and her whole body stiffened. 'What have you given her?'

'Nothing, nothing at all. Look, it had half a mouse earlier. It's probably just bringing that up. Or a fur ball.'

'You've poisoned her!'

'I've done nothing of the sort!'

She pushed Phillip away from the cat with a force that sent him reeling. He managed to recover slightly and grabbed onto her wrist and there they stood for a few seconds, strangely entwined, like two lovers holding hands, swaying, until Mrs Moggeridge broke the link with a strong tug and Phillip lost his balance completely. He staggered backwards, banging his head on the Welsh dresser, and in his few remaining seconds of consciousness tried to grab onto the back of a chair. Instead he seized only air and plunged head first into the cat's water bowl. Mrs Moggeridge was far too busy tending to Virginia to notice his plight. It was only the cat who watched with its bright eyes as Phillip lay unconscious, face down in the bowl, water filling his lungs. And, cradled in protective arms, Virginia seemed to recover briefly from her ailment to glance back at the drowning man with a look of curiosity, followed by satisfaction.

# The Story of Jane who got Carried Away with Plastic Surgery:
# A Cautionary Tale for Adults

Anne-Marie Norman

A girl called Jane lived on the Downs,
In one of those quaint Sussex towns,
Despite a home that was ideal,
She wasn't courteous or genteel.

Her parents, to improve Jane's knowledge,
Had sent her to a ladies' college,
They gave her everything and more,
Perhaps that was their only flaw.

*Anne-Marie Norman*

In Jane's class were fifteen teens,
All desperate to be beauty queens,
The school held beauty pageants yearly,
'Twas all quite superficial really.

Now Jane had never won the prize;
She wasn't the right shape or size,
And since she'd no goodwill or grace,
It was reflected in her face.

Kushelle was prettiest of the girls;
All blue eyes and gold hair in curls,
An hourglass figure all admired,
Straight teeth to which they all aspired.

Kushelle was tipped to win the crown,
So on the field Jane pushed her down,
She bruised her legs with little kicks,
And beat her arms with hockey sticks.

Back home Jane found her mother cooking,
'Mama, I know that I'm good looking',
She said, 'But I must be the best,
To win the beauty queen contest.'

'I'm going to have some liposuction,
Breast implants and a nose reduction,
Oh pretty please, oh sweet mama,
I'll need your credit card and car.'

## The Story of Jane who got Carried Away with Plastic Surgery

'But dear,' her mother said, 'you're young,
You're seventeen and highly strung,
You've grandma's ears and father's nose.'
Cried Jane, 'I have no need of those!'

She snatched her mother's bag and drove,
To a clinic outside Hove,
Wherein a doctor and a nurse,
Relieved her of her coat and purse.

The surgeon said he'd make Jane fit,
Like Marilyn, Raquel and Brigitte,
Or like a model on the telly,
Or that sketch by Botticelli.

His résumé was most amazing;
Degrees in dance and double glazing,
He'd bought them in a sale online,
Two for nine pounds ninety-nine.

Into theatre Jane was wheeled,
How she fussed and swore and squealed!
Until they gave her anaesthetic,
Which made her much less energetic.

They sucked the fat clean out of Jane,
And then they put some back again,
Into bottom, lips and cheeks,
She'd not smile or sit down for weeks.

*Anne-Marie Norman*

With implants Jane's new size would be,
A forty-two quadruple 'G',
The surgeon measured them and said,
'They're four times bigger than her head!'

But a mix up at the factory meant,
That where the saline usually went,
They'd been pumped full of helium gas,
The surgeon didn't check, alas!

When she awoke Jane was feeling,
Somewhat closer to the ceiling,
She tiptoed lightly out the door,
Her feet had hardly touched the floor.

And as she walked down Brighton Pier,
Taking in the atmosphere,
A sudden breeze caught her off guard,
She grabbed on to the railings hard.

Her hands became so very sore,
She couldn't hold on any more,
A gust of wind filled up her coat,
She let go and began to float!

Over boats and coastal skippers,
Nudist beaches, skinny dippers,
On a continental course;
There was no time to feel remorse.

*The Story of Jane who got Carried Away with Plastic Surgery*

Mama sent Jane her old passport,
By carrier pigeon; a nice thought,
But Jane's photo now won't match her face,
No use when entering French airspace!

Without 'sat nav' or modern mapping,
You'll see her not waving but flapping,
To stay above sharks and piranhas,
That girl looks like she's gone bananas!

So if nothing's in her way,
She might have got to St Tropez,
Or she might be further still,
In Zanzibar or West Brazil.

And after winter's bitter freezes,
Come warmer climes and southern breezes,
Her parents hope that in the spring,
She'll turn around and float back in.

The moral of this story's plain,
Don't be jealous, mean or vain,
For what goes up always descends,
And sharks are never far, my friends.

# Bernie and Me at the Movies

Bob Glaberson

Bernie was as impressed by Belmondo as I was. I said something a little derogatory once about Belmondo's swagger but Bernie's response was, 'I could do with a little of that myself.' That spoke volumes. Bernie was overweight and talked almost in a whisper.

We both worked during the day in the midtown area, so we tended to meet in Horn and Hardart's cafeteria on 42$^{nd}$ Street on the east side, just a short walk across town from the movie houses between Broadway and Eighth Avenue. Whoever was the first to arrive would just sit at one of the tables and wait for the other. We never planned to have dinner there but if one or both of us felt like it we would get something and eat it. Sometimes we were eating at the same time.

As we ate our H&H special baked beans in a pot we would have the New York Post opened to the movie page in front of us.

'Hey, there's another Belmondo flick on at the Lyric,' one of us would say.

*Bernie and Me at the Movies*

We sat there in the movie house and lapped it up, Belmondo's amazing success with women and by the time the film was over and we hit the street there was a spring in both of our steps. Belmondo had done something for both of us. I think we both felt that we had lived a little through him.

Bernie was this very square-shaped, bearded person who walked with a little waddle. After catching a couple of flicks together we just got into this habit of meeting up at the H&H every Tuesday night for a movie.

On Tuesdays I normally waited for Bernie, as he had further to walk than me; I would read the paper while waiting and look up films to see what was good. When Bernie arrived he would almost always start the conversation by saying:

'Is there anything good on?'

'John Wayne?'

'I would settle for John Wayne.' Or he would come in and I would say, 'Alan Ladd?'

He would usually just nod. We lived in this heightened world together and when the movie was over, after walking a few blocks we would often go into a local diner and sit opposite each other at one of the tables and re-play the movie.

I would sometimes tell Bernie about the women I was dating. His eyes lit up when I told him some of the stories about them but more often than not I was telling about the women I wished I was dating. Once at the automat he said to me after a girl with a trolley had just come along to clean the plates off our table:

'That girl with the trolley, I could go for her.'

This was a rather round Latin looking woman with long straight hair tied together with a band.

'Well, now's your chance,' I said. He grinned.

'I got an idea.' I said. 'Let's go get some more beans and then wait for the girl to come by again and clear the table and this time have something ready to say.'

Bernie was still grinning but it was a fixed grin.

I made as if to go get some more beans.

'No, no,' he said urgently and tugged at my sleeve for me to sit down.

It was then I realized just how scared Bernie was.

'Okay,' I said, wanting to help, 'I'll start the conversation then you can join in.'

Bernie just sat there looking square and sweating a little.

'Okay, Okay,' I said, taking up the paper and staring at the movie page. 'Paul Newman,' I sighed.

Bernie shook his head up and down vigorously and his grin turned into a happy smile.

'Okay,' I said to him, 'tonight we're going to live a little.'

# Henry In School and Out

Bob Glaberson

Henry was in our class; he was a bit slow. He was always sleepy in school. I remember him leaning his bespectacled head against another boy's in a school photo.

His parents were always worried about him.

'Thank you for looking after him,' they said.

His mother always had one hand clasped in the other like she was praying.

'Thank you for taking Henry camping. Thank you for taking Henry shopping,' she would say.

His father was always in his study working. I hadn't seen him since the day he yelled at Henry for making spelling mistakes. His father was a lawyer. I think there was a lot of disappointment there. Whenever the father appeared the mother's shoulders fell.

'Henry's doing fine at the supermarket,' his mother said. 'He's keeping the shelves full aren't you Henry?'

Henry beamed at her.

'Good going Henry,' I said.

I said to her, 'it looks like Henry's making a success of his life.'

'Tell that to his father,' she whispered.

Out there in the wood Henry was real good at picking up sticks. I let him light the first match and up the fire would leap igniting some of the twigs of an overhanging tree. I read stories to Henry around the campfire as did the others from our class.

Henry was a bit slow so I guess I sort of forgot about him. When I try to remember him though, I get warm feelings. Just think all this time I could have been taking Henry camping.

# Manna from Heaven

Bob Glaberson

Blackie had a drink problem. One day his wife got angry and kicked him out. Blackie was at his wits end, stumbled out into the street in need of a shave, and threw his arms up to heaven;

'Lord,' he said, 'I throw myself on your mercy.' At that moment through his outstretched hands he could see a baby hurtling toward him from out of the sky.

Blackie had just enough time to catch the baby who had fallen six floors because he had put his weight on a rotten window frame which had fallen out.

For about three minutes Blackie didn't move; he just held on tight to the baby. By that time the hysterical mother was in the street. Blackie let go with reluctance. The mother even had to pry some of Blackie's fingers loose from the baby before she could regain control of her child.

Blackie had found the purpose of his life in the life of that little baby. He visited the family of the child and over the years became a kind of unofficial godfather to him, looking after him, taking him to the park and always solicitous of his well-being, so much so that he figured he had to make changes in his own life in order to be of help to the child, who grew up more or less as his son as the father eventually disappeared. Blackie stopped drinking and was able to go back home with his wife who eventually gave birth to two kids herself. Then Blackie was able to be a father to his own children too.

# So This is It?

Bob Glaberson

So this is what it feels like to be dead. Not that much different to be honest. I was sad for all those gathered round my bed; my heart went out to my children, their eyes were like raw eggs looking up at me. My own childhood came back to me and I was sad there as well. I don't know why because my childhood wasn't sad it was chaotic.

Those gardens we used to play in, the hide and seek and Francho out of sight in the rose bushes. Francho actually came to look for me in the hospital but it was too late. He was grey by then and he just seemed to sag when he got there and found everyone sitting there looking at my corpse.

Oh sadness, there's wells of it. That's what seems to seep out of life when it's almost gone. It is all hurtling away so fast. Life? What is it? Just a leaf that's dissolved. I'm sad just looking back at myself dashing around taking it seriously.

There was another dead guy in the bus taking us away from the life world.

'Life means so much and it's sad,' I said to him. 'I felt sad before I died, just moments before.'

'Yeah, it's funny,' the guy said. 'The living take it seriously. They can't help it.'

I said: 'Yeah, we all did, and yet look at it. It's just a pinprick, fast disappearing.'

We just had to laugh.

# Christmas at Aunt Delphie's

Deborah Waldon

Christmas at Aunt Delphie's was always something special; you see she had these dolls, antique dolls. Every room in the house, yes even the smallest room, had at least one doll.

To Aunt Delphie they were her babies; quite an insult to her real babies despite the fact that *they* were full grown.

Cousins Angela, Monica and Michael were all embarrassed by their mother's obsession. That she collected dolls wasn't the problem; no, the problem was that she talked to them, invited them to every meal (though the dolls sometimes politely declined) and introduced them to visitors.

At Christmas all the dolls were required to attend the main festivities in the old ballroom. Each doll would spend the period in the run up to Christmas with Mr Perkins. Mr Perkins was a doll maker and repairer; though Aunt Delphie preferred to think of his workshop as either a hospital or beauty salon. The assessment of each doll would begin in earnest in September when Aunt Delphie, Mr Perkins and his daughter Daisy, the doll's dressmaker, would spend many an hour enjoying tea and cake in the company of one or more of the dolls.

Aunt Delphie would have noted any little requirement each doll had and would point these out to Mr Perkins. These would be along the lines of 'eyes: not as bright as usual', 'dress: a tad the worse for wear' etcetera.

Come Christmas Eve every doll would be resplendent and would be present in the ballroom for the Henslowe Hall Christmas Ball.

The Ball would be attended by all the family; Angela, her husband Peter and their son Toby; Monica, her husband Antony and the twins Clarissa and Clementine. Michael would come alone, more often than not, or occasionally with a special friend. This year his special friend was Stephen.

Then my Mother and Father would arrive with me in tow. I would be sitting in the back of the motor car dreading the ordeal to come. All those people to meet and greet. If it wasn't for the dolls this would have been intolerable.

Of course the great and the good of the neighbourhood would be invited too and many would attend; most out of a sense of duty to the family, many others out of curiosity to see inside the Hall and for a chance to be presented to the dolls.

The ballroom would be decorated with swathes of greenery brought in from the garden. Candles would be dotted around the room, though fewer now than there used to be; children could no longer be trusted to behave themselves and there were too many priceless antiquities to chance; not to mention the problems should some little Johnny or Mary burn a hole in their clothes.

*Christmas at Aunt Delphie's*

Without a doubt the last of the party to arrive would be Mr Perkins and his daughter Daisy. Mr Perkins would wear the same suit every year and every year the patches on the knees and elbows and seat would be shinier and shinier.

Daisy, by contrast, would look her finest. Each year she would take inspiration from one of the dolls and design and make her own dress for the ball.

This year she took inspiration from a doll that carried the title of The May Queen. The May Queen's own dress was of palest green satin embroidered with wild flowers. Daisy's dress was of a darker green satin embroidered with Christmas roses.

Daisy, though in her thirties, was a simple woman. She took delight in twirling around the room showing off her handiwork and posing for an occasional photographic portrait with The May Queen.

I would take refuge at the farthest end of the room, alone with two or three dolls for company, and try to hide as much as I could. This wasn't as easy as you may think. My Mother, miffed at the attention Daisy received, would try to coax me out from hiding to introduce me to someone or other she thought it 'worth knowing'. Often this would be a young man or the parents of a young man Mother would deem 'suitable'.

This year was no exception. Mother introduced me to Dr and Mrs Smethwick and their son William. I agreed to a dance with William under the watchful eyes of the assembled guests, the dolls and the oily stares of the ancestors.

The evening wore on and William and I danced on, his hand warm and firm on my back. The murmur of the human audience grew as William and I took obvious delight in each other's company.

The non-human audience took up a murmuring of their own. I looked to the bay window where Daisy sat watching my every move. As William spun me round my eyes met with the eyes of all the dolls. I was sure each of the dolls was watching me and did not like what they saw.

I tried to force my eyes away from theirs and back to the loving warmth of William's but the murmurs of the dolls increased. I looked to William for signs that he was as concerned as I was as the volume of the dolls murmurs drowned out the sounds from the humans, from the music. But William showed no signs that anything was amiss.

I managed to mutter to William that perhaps we should break from dancing and take some refreshment. Immediately the noise ceased. I excused myself and made for the lavatory. The coolness of the room was a relief. I looked to the window ledge expecting to see one of the dolls but realised that, of course, all the dolls were within the ballroom.

I took some time about my toilet, dressing my hair and smoothing my clothes. Slowly the beating of my heart resumed its more usual pace and I braced myself to venture out of the safety I felt in this most normal of activities to the unexplained phenomenon of the ballroom.

As I opened the lavatory door I was startled by Daisy. She stood as close to the door as to suggest her ear had been pressed against it. Her look pierced through to my very soul. Her eyes were glassy, her smile fixed, her skin waxy.

I pushed past her and fled along the corridor. As I reached the doors to the ballroom, my heart once again pounding, I hesitated. Inside would be the familiar faces of my family, the acquaintances I met each Christmas and William. There would also be the dolls.

I turned my head and saw Daisy lumbering towards me. Her limbs appeared to be slightly stiffened. I pushed open the doors, closed them firmly behind me and made my way to William. He smiled as he saw me approach and held up a glass of Champagne. I took it in both hands and gulped it down. Out of the corner of my eye I tried to surmise the mood of the dolls but they looked as they had before, just dolls.

Suddenly the doors to the ballroom burst open and Daisy stood framed in the doorway. All eyes turned to her. The music stopped abruptly. Daisy's stiff waxy limbs moved spasmodically as she entered the room, her gaze fixed upon me. The assembled crowd watched, transfixed, as she made her way rigidly towards me. No one moved; each person held firmly by the horror before them.

As she closed the gap between us, every person in the room was powerless to stop her; unwilling, unable to move. I felt my throat constrict as though my heart had moved up, blocking the flow of air, suffocating me. Daisy's stiff arms reached for my throat. A squeak escaped my lips.

The dolls took up their previous murmuring and their eyes followed Daisy's progress; their expression seeming to approve of Daisy intentions.

A movement from the far end of the room forced my gaze away from Daisy. Mr Perkins was walking toward us. As he reached his daughter his hand touched the back of her head and Daisy turned to him. Mr Perkins took hold of her hand and led her away, past the statuesque assembly, through the doors by which she'd entered, away into the night.

As the grandfather clock in the hall started to chime midnight, the spell was broken and gradually all returned to their cheery Christmas selves. All except me.

Though no one seems to have any memory of those strange events that night much has changed. Aunt Delphie has given away all of her dolls. Mr Perkins and Daisy have not been heard of again. And never mentioned.

My daughter plays with fluffy doggies, bunnies and bears. No doll has ever entered our house.

# Funny Turn

Deborah Waldon

Thirty six years I've lived in the same house. I've explored every crevice. I replaced the skirting in the dining room. The kitchen's been completely gutted twice; once when I won the pools and then again eight years ago after the fire.

I got housewives knee through cleaning the floors. I got an electric shock from the bad wiring in the bathroom. The fireplace in the living room was boarded up in the seventies and exposed again in the nineties. There used to be three bedrooms and a bathroom. Now there are two bedrooms, one with an en suite, and a guest bathroom.

What's now the en suite was the nursery where I spent hours on end nursing my little ones for the first six years of our marriage.

Anna was very poorly when we first brought her home. They didn't have the intensive care for babies then that they have now. I prayed through the night on more than one occasion those first few months. You should see her now though. She's a wonderful mother and a fabulous wife to David.

Jack was robust. That's the only word for it; robust. Nothing ever knocked him for six. Oh he had the occasional cold, the odd sniffle, but that's it. Never had measles, mumps, chicken pox. He seemed to escape it all. Or almost all.

Jenny was a sweetie. Smiled all the time. Never grumbled. Oh you'd get a slight whimper out of her when she was hungry or her nappy needed changing that was it. She still smiles a lot; it's what makes her so good in a courtroom. The ones in the witness box trust her and they tell her things they shouldn't.

After the kids came Tom and I were so happy. We had everything we could ever have wanted. The house was brand new and the furniture. We felt like kings with all we had.

This house was always lovely, warm and homely. That's what I liked about it. Not now though. Now it's cold. I thought I'd paid it. The central heating's gas but the timer switch is electric. You'd think, having lived here so long, I would know my way around. You'd think I'd remember that dodgy floorboard on the top step but... I was going to say I didn't see it in the dark. But I should have just known it was there. I never normally look even when the lights are on, I just know.

Out there, under the roses, that was our pet cemetery. Hamsters, guinea pigs, cats, goldfish. They're all out there you know. That's probably what makes the roses bloom so well in that spot; all that fertiliser.

Jack had always wanted to be a pilot. Ever since he was a

little boy and we first took him to Biggin Hill. All through school all he used to talk about when he could be a pilot; when he'd be old enough to join up. He was so proud climbing out of his plane after his first flight.

Tom wasn't there that day; I didn't know where he'd got to. Couldn't imagine. Why would he miss his son's first flight? His only son and heir. Told me later that he'd got lost coming from work on the new bypass.

I had the girls with me, they'd not miss something like that; they knew how important it was to Jack.

I should have seen it coming really. He'd never been that into personal appearance or personal hygiene for that matter. Then he comes home with aftershave. I didn't know he knew what aftershave was. Started stinking out the bathroom with Old Spice. Bought himself umpteen new shirts, trousers, ties; his wardrobe was bigger than mine.

That was just the start. Her name was Amanda. He'd see her as often as he could and didn't mind if it was the kids' birthdays, my birthday or Christmas. He was never home now. I was the last one to know, of course, they must all have been talking behind my back. I thought he was just busy at work, like he said. It's hard building up your own business. Even harder when you're never there. When I found out it was the cruellest thing of all. I don't know how he could have done that to me.

Oh my leg hurts. I can't even see if it's bleeding. I've run my hand over it and I can't feel anything sticky or wet but you can never be too sure. It's pitch in here.

When the RAF brought Jack home they did it all properly with the flag and the last post and all that. Then they folded the flag up and gave it to me. I couldn't cry. I couldn't take it all in. Tom said he needed her for support; said he couldn't get through a thing like this without her at his side. Inside I was screaming 'What about me?' Inside the tears were flowing, I was burning up with anger but outside I was calm, placid. Papers hinted that I was cold.

Tom moved out before Jack had been in his grave a week. Anna wanted to move back in with me but the orange blossom was still fresh in her hair. How could she leave David now even for a short while? Jenny was away at university and I wasn't going to have her missing out. That old sod wasn't going to ruin her life too. I told them I'd be all right. Course I wasn't.

The new doctor's given me some pills for the 'blackouts' as he calls them. Funny turns as I call them. I don't think they agree with me.

When I was first alone in the house it seemed so big. I thought I'd move out but I didn't then and later it was handy for when the grandchildren came to stay. I even took in a foreign student once. It was nice having the company but I couldn't understand a word she said.

I know the lights were on last night. I remember turning them off so they must have been on. Today it was so sunny I didn't need any lights and the gas was all right for cooking; I must have paid that. If only I could get to the phone. I've a mobile around here too but I don't know where it is. They're so small these phones now that I can never find it.

It wasn't easy going back to work but I needed the money and the company. Gave me a focus. They were a cheery bunch, always something to laugh about, and on

Fridays we'd go for a drink after work. I was never one for pubs before. When I was a girl they were always for old men, drunks, 'undesirables'. But I got to like them; they're nothing like they were. Well, I expect some are.

Money started getting tight after I lost my job. Gave it to some young kid fresh out of school. I always liked typing but the new computers threw me. I shouldn't begrudge that kid a job but the pension doesn't go far.

Mrs Lacey's usually home by now. If I bang on the wall I'm sure she'll hear me. 'Mrs Lacey. Mrs Lacey.' Course her name's Amanda too.

# I Killed My Grandad

Deborah Waldon

**Monday**

When I close my left eye, I can see my pirate ship. When I close my right eye I can't see it. My arm feels funny.

I want to get up and go downstairs. I want my breakfast. I like Coco pops. I like lots of milk with my Coco pops, then the milk goes brown.

But I can't go downstairs. I killed my Grandad. I didn't mean to do it, it was an accident. Now Mummy doesn't like me. I don't want to go downstairs.

I hear my Daddy call me. I have to get up now.

I get up and Daddy takes me downstairs. Mummy's crying. There are flowers on the table. Maybe it's Mummy's birthday today, that's when Daddy buys her flowers. I should have made her a card. There are lots of cards already. They say sorry and another word with S.

Mummy doesn't look at me. She must be very, very mad at me. I killed her Daddy and I didn't make her a card.

Daddy says we haven't got any Coco pops. I have egg

and soldiers. Daddy says I'm a soldier too. Daddy says I don't have to go to school today so I just eat my soldiers.

Daddy says he's taking me for a ride in the car. Daddy says Mummy wants to be on her own.

We go in Daddy's car. We go to the hospital where Grandad was. Daddy talks to some people and then they give him a box. Daddy puts the box in the car next to my car seat. In the box I can see Grandad's jumper.

Daddy is sad. He doesn't talk to me. He looks like he's going to cry but he doesn't cry.

Then we to go to the shops. We get Coco pops and pizza and meat and apples and other things. Daddy buys ice cream. He says that it's for me, if I'm a good boy. I'm not a good boy. I don't know if I can have ice cream.

When we get home, Mummy's not crying now but she doesn't look at me. She pats me on the head. Daddy and me put the shopping away. Then I go to my room and I play.

We have pizza. Daddy says we have to eat salad with pizza. It's going to make me strong. I don't like salad. I put lots of mayo on it. Daddy doesn't talk much. Mummy doesn't eat anything. Daddy gives me ice cream anyway even though I'm not a good boy. Maybe he forgot.

**Tuesday**
Mummy and Daddy have to go out. I have to stay with Mrs Graham. It smells funny at Mrs Graham's house. She doesn't have any toys to play with. I have my pirate ship and Jack Sparrow and more pirates and I have my cars with me.

I have lunch with Mrs Graham. We have cheese sandwiches and crisps. Mrs Graham doesn't make me eat salad. I drink orange but it's not juice, it's funny stuff that Mrs Graham puts in a glass with water. I don't want to stay here anymore.

I can't tell Mrs Graham that I killed my Grandad. She says my mummy is sad. She says I have to be a good boy for Mummy.

Mummy and Daddy come late. It's dark when we get to our house. Mummy goes to bed, she doesn't talk to me. Daddy gives me McDonalds and hot chocolate. I watch my DVD and then I go to bed.

## Wednesday

We don't go out today. We all stay at home. Mummy talks on the phone lots and lots. Daddy says she is talking to Aunty Kathy. Mummy cries on the phone. I watch TV. I watch DVDs and I eat spaghetti on toast for lunch.

At night Mummy goes to bed before me. Daddy and me have meat and potatoes and carrots.

## Thursday

I want to go to school today. I miss my friends. Daddy says I can go to school. I can go to school with Sam and his daddy. At school Mrs Andrews says am I all right. Sam and Sunita and George play with me. We learn about telling the time.

Sunita says when we die we come back then we're animals or birds. That's what Sunita's mummy says too. Sunita's mummy and daddy have different gods. Sunita's daddy says people don't come back as animals and birds. He says it's silly. But Sunita says it's true.

Sam says people go to heaven when they die.

*I Killed My Grandad*

George says people die, then they come back and they are ghosts and they come and get you. George says that ghosts can kill you and walk through walls and make funny noises at night.

I don't know where my Grandad has gone. I didn't tell them that I killed my Grandad.

★★★

When we went to Grandad's house before, Mummy and Daddy said I had to be good. They said I mustn't upset Grandad because he was very sick. Mummy went to Grandad's kitchen and did the washing and made lunch. Daddy went in the garden and cut down the dead tree. Daddy said I had to stay out the way cos he had a big electric saw thing.

Me and Grandad were in the living room. Grandad asked me about my school. I told him I have lots of friends at school. Grandad asked me about my swimming class. I told Grandad I can't swim yet. Grandad laughed at me, he said I was a sissy. I'm not a sissy. Grandad said I'm a girl. I got mad at Grandad and I shouted at him. Grandad laughed. Then he coughed. He didn't stop coughing. Then he touched his arm. Then he fell down.

Mummy came into the living room with lunch on a tray. She saw Grandad on the floor. She asked me what happened but I didn't say anything. Mummy knelt on the floor with Grandad. Then Mummy asked on the phone for an ambulance. Then an ambulance came. They took Grandad to the hospital. I killed my Grandad.

★★★

When I got home from school I read to Daddy. We have fish fingers. Mummy eats some fish fingers. She's not crying today.

**Friday**
I go to school again today. Daddy takes me and Sam. We sit together in Daddy's car.

At school we do sums. We do reading. I like reading.

We have sausages and chips and beans. Then we have sponge pudding with custard.

Today Sunita has a tummy upset and her mummy comes and she goes home.

Daddy and me watch TV. Mummy watches TV for a bit then she goes to have a bath.

**Saturday**
Mummy and Daddy say we have to go to Grandad's house today. I don't want to go into Grandad's house. What if Grandad is a ghost now and he's in the house?

Mummy says I can play in the garden. Mummy and Daddy go in the house. I play in the garden by myself. It's nice in Grandad's garden. There are gnomes in the garden. Grandma liked gnomes. Grandma died when I was a baby. There are lots of flowers in the garden. Red ones and yellow ones and white ones and blue ones.

I play at the bottom of the garden a long way away from Grandad's house.

Then it starts to rain and Mummy comes to the door

and she says I have to come in now. I don't want to go indoors. I don't look at Mummy. Mummy calls me again. She says I have to come indoors because of the rain.

I go into Grandad's house. Mummy puts the lights on. I can't see Grandad's ghost.

Then there is a funny noise. I'm scared. Mummy asks me what's wrong. I don't talk to Mummy.

Daddy asks me if I'm all right. I don't know what to say so I nod my head.

Mummy and Daddy have a cup of tea and I have an orange juice. Aunty Kathy comes and Mummy and Aunty Kathy hug and cry. I don't know if Aunty Kathy knows that I killed Grandad.

Aunty Kathy gives me a hug but she's still crying and doesn't talk. Then she hugs Daddy.

Mummy and Aunty Kathy go upstairs.

Daddy says I can help him. We go into the garage and we put all Grandads' things in boxes.

Later we go home and we have Chinese food from the shop. Aunty Kathy stays in our house.

## Sunday

Today I wake up. I hear Mummy go into Aunty Kathy's room. I go to Aunty Kathy's bedroom door. I see Mummy and Aunty Kathy in bed eating toast and drinking tea. I want to go in but I can't.

I go downstairs. I want my breakfast but I can't find Daddy. I stand on a chair and I get the Coco pops. Then I get the milk from the fridge. I eat my Coco pops.

# The Last Will and Testament of William Morris Thackery Shakespeare de Witt

Deborah Waldon

My last will and testament
The last thing I will write
I'm leaving all my worldly goods
To Stephen Francis Sprite.

I'm lying on my deathbed
I've nothing more to add
For when you see what's writ below
You'll know I wasn't mad.

My parents up and left me
When I was just eighteen
The only contact now we have
Is in their mausoleum.

Off I went to Cambridge
Off I went alone
I didn't understand the boys
I never felt at home.

*The Last Will and Testament*

And then one day I saw him
When I was off to bed
Stephen Francis in my room
Standing on his head.

He told me all his stories
Of his life of derry do
We finished all the gin I had
And all the whisky too.

Money was no object
I bought all he desired
In old Cambridge town he was
The very best attired.

Yellow leather jerkins
And garters for his socks
On a winter's eve he had
A stole made out of fox.

The boys they couldn't see
What I saw in Mr Sprite
The profs they asked sotto voiced
If I was quite all right.

The matron gave me castor oil
A dose would do me good
A punt along the Cam, I thought
Was better for my mood.

*Deborah Waldon*

All throughout the war
He did stay right by my side
At the altar there he was
When I took me a bride

The last thing I do see
As I gaze upon the chair
Is Stephen's best top hat to know
That he was ever there.

# Reunion

Deborah Waldon

'I can't believe it's you,' we said.

We both stopped in our tracks and looked at each other, examining each other in detail.

We sat at a table and talked as our teas, strong with a dash of milk and one sugar, grew cold.

We compared notes on our childhoods. You fell off your bike when you were five and still have the scar on your left knee to prove it.

I fell out of a tree when I was five and still have the scar on my left knee to prove it.

For your eighth birthday you were given a book called My Family and Other Animals by Gerald Durrell and you developed a fascination for the world around you.

I loved all the David Attenborough programmes that the BBC ever showed and grew to love the world around me.

You were allergic to cream and strawberries although your mother said she couldn't imagine summer without them.

Milk and dairy food made me sick and I came out in spots when I ate strawberries. My mum said milk was good for me and didn't know what to do. She said strawberries were overpriced and overrated.

For your ninth birthday you were given a professional microscope and a butterfly net.

For my tenth birthday I was given a second-hand children's microscope that came in a box with some pieces missing. And my brother bought me a 50p fishing net from a shop at the beach.

Your father built a shed for you in your garden in Melbourne with electricity for heat, light and incubators, *and* running water, for you to use as your lab.

My mum took me to the library every Saturday to borrow books about animals and insects. Once a year, as a birthday treat, we got on the train at Hastings and went to the Natural History Museum in London.

You fell in love for the first time when you were seventeen to a man who wanted to be a doctor.

I fell in love for the first time when I was seventeen to a girl who worked in Woolies.

Your parents were happy to pay for your study of zoology at The University of Melbourne where you'd still be close to home and they could visit you whenever they wanted.

My dad was willing to put in a good word for me and get me a job in the factory where he worked.

You wanted to travel to Cambridge University in the UK. By now you had discovered your birth certificate that gave your name, not as Kelly Fiona Oberman, but as Fiona MacDonald.

I worked hard to get my scholarship to Cambridge; the first person in my family to go to university. I was worried it would be full of toffs but it was the same college David Attenborough went to.

My dad took on all the overtime he could and put in for promotion to be supervisor of a hundred people, though he was a shy man and would struggle to deal with so many.

My mum took on, as well as her job as a dinner lady, an early morning cleaning job and worked four nights a week in an old folks' home.

My parents had kept my name of Michael MacDonald, was known to my friends as Ronald, but I'd also taken on my new family name of Brown.

My mum said she thought I'd had a twin sister but that she'd died.

One day I typed MacDonald into a genealogy site. I knew nothing of my Scottish heritage and felt a bit of a ponce that I should care - it was all part of the UK after all. But I'd loved Mel Gibson in Braveheart.

You sat at the computer next to mine in the library and I saw you looking up MacDonald tartans on your screen. You had dark brown hair, brown eyes and a snub nose like mine.

Later I saw you in the lab and asked my friend Carol about you. Carol was your lab partner. She couldn't wait to arrange our 'blind date' in the new café at the end of the street, though tried to persuade me to make it somewhere more romantic.

When I arrived I heard a woman at the counter ordering tea with two tea bags left in, a dash of milk and one sugar. And I knew.

# Check the Tides

Helen Bedford

The tides change very fast
In this part of France:
Problem was we didn't know,
Until we realised the fast tide
Was taking us out to sea.

We waved frantically to friends
Watching us from the shore.
They waved back thinking we were having fun
Unaware of the danger we were in
Our desperate situation; what to do.

David always good in a crisis;
First move, took down the sails.
'How do you row?' he asked me.
I can row, but not strong enough,
Gave him a few instructions.

*Check the Tides*

He grabbed the oars and pulled
Soaking me in the icy water.
After a few attempts he got the rhythm,
He's big and strong in mind and body
Pulling hard against the rushing tide.

Noticing the local fishermen
Were following the oyster beds
David made for their direction.
It took half an hour of hard rowing.
It worked, our lives were saved.

We learnt a hard lesson that day;
Always check local tide patterns
Before setting out for a sail.
'Have a lovely sail?' our friends asked,
Totally unaware of our predicament.

# Little Silver Hat

Helen Bedford

There it lay as I opened the drawer;
My little silver hat.
Followed by tears that had never been shed.
What would you like for your birthday, darling ?
I asked weeks before.
Silver hat, hold-ups, glasses, came the cheeky reply.

Our cottage in France, beautiful sunny morn
Into the bathroom I sauntered.
With a seductive walk out I came.
Here comes your birthday present.
Laughter filled the air,
His face alight with Happiness, Joy, Love.

It was his seventieth,
Six months later, my darling gone forever.

# Soul Mates

Helen Bedford

I remember the first time I saw her
standing on the diving board
about to plunge in. I glanced up,
she looked down on me.

My first thoughts: *What a funny little thing;*
*But what magnificent thighs.*
Something drew me to her presence
as she performed a perfect dive.

I'd never seen her at the club before.
After the dive, she ignored me;
the only girl there to do that to me,
which intrigued me all the more.

She disappeared at the end of the evening,
the other girls hanging around the boys.
The following week I trailed her to her bus
and sat next to her – she went red.

*Helen Bedford*

'Coming for a coffee?' I ask.
'No thank you,' she replies.
'Why not?'
'Not with wet hair.'
'I don't mind your wet hair.'

We got down from the bus,
All my pocket money spent on that coffee.
I was fourteen, still at school.
We were both so very young.

She became my best friend:
so easy to be with.
We cycled, swam, rowed on the Thames,
talking constantly to each other;
a closeness that lasted a life-time.

# We Meet Again

Helen Bedford

I was fourteen years old; small for my age, five feet tall, long, naturally blonde hair. Full of life and confidence, as one is at that age, having just begun a five-year apprenticeship as a hairdresser and after a few weeks working in a salon, which I loved. I was very happy there; meeting lots of people, chatting to them, listening to stories about their lives was so interesting, but I felt the need to meet other young people. I started evening classes at a school behind Oxford Street in London, taking Mum and my Aunt as models. Having just returned from being evacuated to the country to avoid the London bombings, my life now changed back to life in the city. The year? 1945.

Asking around I found there was a Youth Club in Kennington Road, which was only one road away from where I lived in Westminster Bridge Road, Lambeth. One evening I decided to walk down to the hall where the youth club was held on Tuesdays. I turned up in a pretty blue dress, my long hair loose and freshly washed. When I walked in I was warmly welcomed by everyone. In no time I was playing table tennis, darts, and the boys showed me how to use a billiard cue. Then on went the record player and some danced to the music. I didn't know how to dance. One friendly girl called Ella took me through the simple steps of the waltz.

She said, 'Once a fortnight we have ballroom dancing lessons. You will soon learn, Helen.' It was such fun that first evening, just being with young people around my own age.

After a couple of weeks one boy, André said, 'Would you like to go to the pictures this coming Saturday? Or any Saturday?'

No boy had ever asked me out before. I felt my face go red with embarrassment.

'I will let you know next week,' I replied.

When I got home I told Mum. 'Shall I go?' I asked her.

'He's a nice boy, isn't he?' mum asked. 'If you like him and want to go, I don't see a problem.'

So the following week I told him I would love to go.

He met me outside the cinema, situated near Victoria Station. He arrived, gave me a box of chocolates and took me into the cinema. After we had sat down he held my hand. I found it a strange experience. After the film he took me to Lyons' Corner House for coffee; a popular venue at that time. We talked; he told me his parents owned a pub in Piccadilly. He was attending the City of Westminster School.

After some weeks of going to the club, one evening a boy walked in whom I had never seen before. How can you explain instant attraction? I found myself drawn to this beautiful young man. Unlike André, who was brown-eyed and had very dark brown hair, about five feet ten inches in height, this boy was an Adonis.

He smiled at me and said; 'Fancy a game of table tennis?'

He was an excellent player and beat me every time. He sat with me and André, and Ella, the first girl to befriend me. We all laughed and chatted together; totally comfortable in each other's company.

During that following week I met him when he was out on his cycle.

'Hello, Helen. Where are you off to?'

'Swimming,' I replied.

'Have you a bicycle? We could go cycling on Sunday.' I was amazed that he asked me.

We met up on the Sunday and cycled to Hyde Park where we had a magical afternoon. We didn't stop talking; we had so much in common. He said he was an athlete and belonged to the London Athletic Club. He also swam, played tennis, cycled, ice skated and danced. The afternoon flew by. He told me he went to Alleyne's College in Dulwich.

We became bosom pals and after a long friendship we eventually married. He was my only true love. André and I remained friends throughout those years.

We would all sometimes go out together; Ellie, David, André, myself. We were all very young just having fun growing up.

## Helen
It was only when I was in the car, actually driving to the ferry at Newhaven that my courage failed.

What on earth have I done? I thought to myself. There was no going back now, the ferry crossing booked, also the overnight stay in Le Mans.

I loved Le Mans, having stayed there so many times in the past: Fun weekends with a group of friends to see the 24-hour race; camping near the straight; wonderful food: Also, on the way down to the Dordogne, it became a 'must' to stay at the Hotel De Ville, a small family-run hotel which we'd got to know well over the years.

Here, I was alone, on a trip to France for the first time since my darling died five years ago. It has taken months to plan this trip; weeks of research to find André after all these years. He had left England at eighteen to go to live with his mother in France to avoid National Service.

Before André went to France we said our goodbyes I said, *One day when we are old, I will find you, as I shall want to know what you did with your life and if you were happy.*

Anyhow, earlier this year I decided to try to track André down. Forty-two years later; knowing it would be a difficult task.

I had only two clues: One was that he did a two-year training course in Hotel Management at the City of Westminster School. His plan? To one day own a hotel in France. The second? He had sent a photograph to Eileen Bennett, a mutual friend, of him mixing cocktails in a hotel bar, in the Loire area of France. That was all I had to go on.

So began the search. He loved the Loire area, so I wrote to the local Town Hall in Amboise for a list of hotels. This was either a lucky break or great intuition, I shall never know which, but back came brochures from the information advice centre in town. I could not believe my eyes, after going through all the brochures, one said: Proprietor, André Slater, Hotel De Vanne. Eureka!!

Then began the planning, which was to book the ferry, book into his hotel under my married name so he would have no clue. Now aged sixty he would not recognise the young girl he once knew. The plan was to stay there and see for myself if he had children, grandchildren. Maybe I would make myself known to him or maybe I wouldn't.

When I told my two sons I was off to France for a few days for a trip down memory lane they thought I was very brave. *Phone us, Mum. Let us know you arrive safely!*

Of course they did not know the object of the exercise.

I drove on to the ferry at Newhaven; the first time I had ventured on such a trip alone. I stood on the deck, the wind blowing my hair; so many memories flooding back. David and I had bought a barn and converted it in the Dordogne. We went to France so often during our marriage, the boys sharing that love.

I had lunch on board and, in no time, the French coast came into view.

The drive down to Le Mans, was a familiar one, having done the journey so many times (I always navigated). Arriving at the Hotel De Ville, I was amazed that the proprietor, now in his seventies, still recognised me. It was six years since my last visit with David.

Bonjour Madame... et Monsieur? He threw his arms up when I told him that he was no longer alive. He kissed me on both cheeks and gave a hug. He called his wife; she had grown old elegantly, her hair now silver. She also hugged and kissed me. They insisted I joined them for supper; a pleasant, nostalgic evening.

I rose early, planning to get on the road, as I had a long drive ahead. The nearer I got to Amboise, the more nervous I felt. What would I find? Will he still be alive?

It was a beautiful sunny day, warm in the May sunshine. I followed the familiar road signs then, suddenly, Amboise, eight kilometres.

When I arrived I parked in the town square; lots of tourists walking around, all there to see the famous château of the area. From enquiring beforehand I knew that the hotel was in the town centre. It is such a beautiful place; full of history and wonderful architecture, the château dominating everything and, of course, the River Loire.

So I wandered around, savouring the ambience. Firstly sitting in the Square for coffee, watching all the smart people doing the same as me, soaking up the atmosphere. Then I said to myself; Come on Helen, don't delay any longer, find the Hotel De Vanne.

It was, as I'd imagined it to be, a very attractive, old, stone building; vines growing up over the walls; tables outside, people sitting under umbrellas, talking, drinking their cognac and coffee. Little girls with their dolls, taking them for a walk around the tables. There is no other atmosphere quite like it anywhere else in the world.

After parking the car nearby I finally walked into the reception lugging my heavy case. A friendly young girl took my name with a smile; *Madame Bedford, welcome.* She tapped the bell; a young man came and took my bag, also with a smile.

I knew at once it was André's son. He looked so much like André when he was young; I guessed he'd be in his mid-twenties. He showed me to my room; typical of a small, comfortable, established, family hotel. Wallpaper covered in roses donned the walls; even on the door panels, which made me smile. A great big oak bed you had to climb to get onto. I bounced up and down on it, knowing I would get a good night's sleep.

The young man said; *My name is André.* Why was I not surprised? *Mine is Helen*, I replied.

## André

I was standing in my usual position on a Saturday afternoon. This is when the new visitors arrived, mostly for short stays. They couldn't see me near the dining room doors, so I could observe without being seen. When this attractive, petite blonde lady booked in at the desk, I noticed her warm smile when she spoke to Michelle, my daughter, and the same smile when she greeted my son, André.

About sixty years old, I mused to myself.

It was three years since my darling died, after a long illness with breast cancer. Life was still very difficult for me with no one to discuss my sorrow. André and Michelle suffered so much; I always put on a bright face for them.

That evening, I noticed Madame Bedford dining alone. She had brought a book with her and read quietly during dinner. After dinner she disappeared to her room. As I see hundreds of new visitors during the year I wondered why this lady caught my interest. There was something about the way she laughed to the waiter. And that amazing smile.

## Helen Bedford

Deep down in my sub-conscience memories stirred of long ago.

The next morning I rose early as I always did to check the kitchens and to discuss the lunch menu with the chef. Going to the market was the thing I liked best; choosing the fruit and vegetables for the day. Then to the boucherie to get the meat, and finally the boulangerie.

I glanced into the garden; someone was already in the pool. I watched with interest. It was Madame Bedford. She climbed out of the water and stood on the one-metre springboard, proceeding to perform an amazingly graceful swallow-dive. She was at one with herself totally unaware that anyone would be watching. Captivated by her diving skills I watched her, forgetting all time.

Finally she took off her swimming cap, shook her blonde hair, which was previously in a bun but I could now see was quite long, and disappeared into the hotel. After breakfast she went out and I did not see her again until dinner. At around nine o'clock she went for a swim. The pool was floodlit; again I watched unseen. After which she went to her room.

When I looked at the hotel register, I saw that her name was Helen. Then of course realisation came in a flash. Helen Bedford. Can it be after forty-two years? Helen, the first girl I had ever asked out. I was so attracted to this tiny ball of fun; full of energy, always smiling, great to be with. Unfortunately she was captivated by another boy at the club so I didn't stand a chance, but we remained good friends until I came to France where my life changed forever; meeting and falling in love with Sophia, now a widower with two super children. Such a co-incidence that she booked into my hotel. I resolved to speak to her that evening.

## Helen

When I walked into the hotel that Saturday I could feel my courage ebbing away. I saw a middle-aged man near the dining room watching visitors book in knowing immediately it was André even after all these years his dark, good looks, thick brown hair and his body language were somehow unchanged. But I did not show that I had either seen him or recognised him.

I also saw him the following morning and evening, watching me swim and dive, but knew if I were patient realisation might come to him.

That evening I dressed with care; my hair freshly washed, my prettiest dress.

He came up to my table and said; *Hello, Helen*, giving a big smile, like his son's.

*Hi André*, I replied.

*What on earth brought you here to France to my hotel?*

One day I may tell him.

He sat down and joined me for dinner. We had a superb meal; melon with ham, boeuf bourguignon and crème brulée, we didn't stop talking; there was forty-two years of life to catch up on.

André told me of his meeting with his wife in Paris; being introduced to her at a party. A beautiful ballet dancer who gave up her career to follow André to the Amboise. She bore him two lovely children; they had twenty-five years of happiness. Sadly, after fighting cancer for two years, she finally died.

It was so painful for him to recall the grief that both he and his children had suffered. He then listened intently whilst I told him about my life with David which was so full and interesting; a closeness only experienced by a few. We had both met soul-mates. It did us so much good, unburdening our hearts to each other. Neither of us had shared our intense sorrow with anybody else. The evening flew by; so much to say. Amazingly, the friendship we'd had in our youth was still there.

The next morning I went for my swim. He came out to join me, saying that he had not been in the pool since Sophia had died. After introducing me properly to his delightful family, with whom I got on well, he invited me to have supper that evening with them in his private apartment. Again, it was a very enjoyable evening; the youngsters were courteous and friendly; they seemed pleased that their father had a friend to talk to. After supper they left us alone to talk. The days flew by.

André took me to the market each morning whilst he shopped for the hotel. French markets are something else, so exciting; cheeses, pâté, fresh mussels, oysters. We stopped at a café for coffee and patisserie, again talking our heads off. Other days we went for walks by the river and visited the châteaux; the days passing until it was time for me to leave. Young André and Michelle seemed to approve of their papa enjoying the company of an old friend.

The morning I was ready to leave, André had croissants and coffee with me, he asked for my address in England. We

*We Meet Again*

hugged and he gently kissed me on both cheeks; a very French gesture. *Goodbye, dear Helen, I will miss you.* He waved me off.

Driving through France I had time to think of the amazing few days, which I had enjoyed so much. On arriving home, my sons phoned to ask how I had enjoyed my break in France. They came to dinner the following evening. I told them what I had done. Surprisingly they were pleased with me.

A couple of weeks went by; I was feeling restless when the phone went.

*Hi Helen*, said a voice down the line. It was André. *I miss you so much. Would you consider coming again soon? Michelle and André liked you a lot and would also love to see you again.*

I chatted it over with the boys. *Do you mind if I go again for a few weeks?*

*Go ahead, Mum; it's your life to enjoy whilst you are fit and well.*

So, off I went, back to Amboise to spend time with André and his family. We really did get on so well. André and I found time to go out alone together; going to restaurants, drives in the beautiful countryside, enjoying each other's company.

After a few weeks I said, *I really must return home.*

Then André said, *Helen, I want you to stay. You have brought sunshine back into my life, which I never thought would happen again. Do you feel the same?*

We were so lucky to be content in each other's company; at the same time knowing it would never be the same we'd had with our first loves. We were content to accept a very friendly and happy companionship.

Ashley and Nicholas came to our wedding. They liked André and his children: in fact, Nicholas seems to be more interested in Michelle; who knows what will happen there!

André and I felt we were so lucky to have found happiness again. I finally told him that it was not fate that brought us together that day.

# Winter Snow

Helen Bedford

Aware that snow was falling gently outside,
White powder slowly covering the hills beyond,
Children will soon arrive, laughter filling the air,
Whizzing down on toboggans and trays
Before the snow has barely time to settle.

As I gazed at the changing scene,
My heart, frozen, heavy with sorrow,
Thoughts of past winters of fun,
Our own children joining the merry scene.
Today, surrounded by loving family, friends:
I bury my darling with leaden heart.

# What Would I Do to Protect the One I Love?

Jenufa Harris

I would protect you, and myself, from the reality that being married to each other is a nightmare. I would not upset you with my unhappiness in case you are infuriated by my demands. I would try to keep you happy and tell you the things you want to hear so that you will not leave me. I would not only lie but I would live a lie; smile when I want to scream, listen to you politely when I am sighing inside at your arrogance, your heartlessness.

When you come home at midnight saying that you have been working late, I will not mention that I rang up your office hours ago and there was no reply. I will push to the back of my mind the questions that are raised by the smell of whisky in the back of your car, the hair clip with a flower on it, which is not mine. The new socks that you took out of the packet and wore for the first time in the morning which somehow turned inside out by the evening.

*What Would I Do to Protect the One I Love?*

Wide eyed, naive, I believe your explanations, and yet there is a deep understanding in my heart that I lie to you and to myself. I pretend that I am ignorant of your deceptions, that we are safe, secure; we have a nice life together. I protect you, your pride, your self-belief so that you will not leave me, I am afraid of being left alone with two children - what would I do?

So I don't throw saucepans, although I feel such rage, have such a powerful desire to throw something at you but no, I don't shout at you, I don't answer back – perhaps I am the worse deceiver, because you have no idea how my love for you is steadily turning into hate.

I am biding my time, knowing this truce is deadly. It feels like war, when the German soldiers played football with the English Tommies on Christmas Eve, right next to the trenches, hoping perhaps that something would happen to stop them killing each other in the morning.

But tomorrow comes, and you announce coldly that you are leaving me, to be with her. The tears begin to drip down my face; not because I love you and my heart is broken but for the loss, the failure, for the waste of years when I loved you and you did not love me back.

I say, 'Yes, it should have happened years ago,' and you look startled, clearly expecting me to cling to your legs wailing, begging you to stay, but I smile at the same time as I cry, I don't cling.

Later that day as you stand at the front door with your bag of clothes and your computer in its box, you say in final parting; 'well, the sex was always good wasn't it?'

I miss my opportunity to tell you the truth for once,

without fear, but protecting you out of habit, or perhaps out of what vestige of love is left, say quietly, 'yes,' and shut the door.

# The Tartan Blanket

Jenufa Harris

He would sit on the same wooden chair, in the same place by the table, while his wife bustled about chatting, criticizing the neighbours or other family members and told him what jobs needed doing or whether he should get ready to go to the bowling green or not, depending on the weather. Sometimes he leaned forward, smiling at his little granddaughter, and he would clasp his hands together with the thumbs side by side, blowing to make owl noises which were sometimes successful sometimes not.

He had a shed in the garden where he did carpentry making a beautiful bookcase or perhaps an ironing board or repairs to shoes. His granddaughter would crouch on the shed floor and hammer nails into lumps of wood to make boats.

Often he would take her with him to the bowling green walking there along the promenade. Not hand in hand but side by side, slowly in silence, she skipping sometimes when she forgot herself. He would meet other elderly men who he knew would stop to say, 'good morning,' tip their caps, and enquire after the health of each other's wives.

Once he said to his acquaintances, proudly, 'this is my granddaughter!'

And the group of old men looked down at her seriously.

She looked up at their faces, their tweedy jackets, their gnarled hardworking hands with hard tendons and blue veins.

'A bonny lass' said one of the men.

Grandfather took his own bowls to the bowling green in a box held under his arm. The game was his one pleasure; he never went to a pub or seemed to have any other interest outside the house. While he played bowls his granddaughter would sit on the little kerb at the edge of the perfect grass and watch as the balls rolled back and forth, heard the deep clunk as they tapped each other.

Often she would wander off and crawl into the neat bushes which surrounded the green, squeezing between the sharp branches and looking for lost coins or crawling right around the edge, out of sight, sitting in the dust and watching her grandfather.

One day she went into the grounds man's hut which was full of bowls on racks and which had a large lawnmower in the corner. The grounds man gave her bowls to play with. She sat on the floor trundling them up and down, a game which seemed to go on for a long time but she didn't know how to end it or politely say 'thank you I'm going now'.

The sun blazed hot outside the hut as the grounds man watched her.

Then her grandfather walked in, looked at the scene, 'Get up,' he said. She scrambled to get up, her bony knees scraping on the wooden floor and went to his side, knowing that somehow she had done something wrong but not understanding exactly what that was.

They walked home together.

Nothing was said yet she knew she had disappointed him and this was how she learned the language of glances, the intimidation of silences, the nuances of gestures, it was an inherited family skill.

The years passed she became a teenager and her mother took her to live her miles away with a new stepfather. She was told that her grandfather was ill in hospital, he had had a stroke.

She cycled with her boyfriend to visit him. They sat by the bed, grandfather in his striped pyjamas, unable to talk. He had a paper and pencil in his hands, struggling to write something. His writing was old fashioned copperplate, shaky, so that she couldn't understand what it said.

Many years later she would think of that scrap of paper with the scrawled writing on it, and remember how lightly she had dismissed it, left it on the bed as she called 'bye Pop, see you soon', and walked away.

He died two days later.

She was given his small signet ring in the shape of a heart which, about a year later, she lost.

Her grandmother had his shed knocked down and gave his bowls to one of his acquaintances.

One thing that did survive was a woven Scottish tartan blanket which had been on his bed for as long as his granddaughter could remember. He had always slept in the small box bedroom at the back of the house on his own. The room was practical, clean and spartan. When she herself was an elderly woman she would hold the itchy blanket to her face and tell him that she loved him and she was strengthened by how very close they had been.

# Electricity

Karen Antoni

Miss Rose had strong arms. She needed them. She carried jugs of water up and down the stairs for mistress to be able to have a wash every morning. Cleanliness is next to godliness thought Miss Rose as she emptied the remains of the water into the bowl.

Most of the servants bathed once a week downstairs. Being the head housemaid Miss Rose had hers on a Friday night in a hip bath in her own room. Certain privileges came with her job; one of these was that she had her own room. At forty one she had been in service for eighteen years. Married to her job, she sighed, as she picked up Lady Ellen Storringtons' chamber-pot and carried it to the bedroom door.

There had been someone once; Joseph was her sweetheart. They had planned to marry after the war but that was never to be. He never came back. And Lady Ellen Storrington had lost her dear beloved grandson, Thomas, a young corporal officer. Twenty two, he had died as a result of injuries which got worse with a bronchial infection. He had been asthmatic as a child. So Thomas didn't stand a chance.

Miss Rose's sister, May, used to be in service but she emigrated to Australia. The family she was in service with moved there to set up some sort of trading business. She could have stayed here at home with excellent references or moved away with the family as a 'maid of all.' May decided to travel with the family. She was young and spirited with a great sense of adventure.

Rose smiled as she remembered the last time she and May had been together five years ago. It had been a hot sunny Sunday, their day off, and they had gone down to the seafront to have a picnic. Take in the sea air. May had brazenly stripped off to her undergarments and gone in the sea. She had walked right in until the sea was up to her torso and then she had jumped and gone right under for at least a minute, totally immersing herself in the sea water.

When she came up her hair was all dripping, her clothes all transparent and clinging to her body. How she had laughed, like a banshee, and yelled, 'come on in Rose, the water's lovely. They can't take this away from us,' and with that she had splashed and kicked the water like a mermaid. If such a thing existed.

Miss Rose had only dared to paddle to just below her knees. 'I didn't know you could swim,' cried Miss Rose.

'Nor did I,' replied May. How they laughed.

She missed May and looked forward to her next letter. May had only been in Australia six months when May wrote and told her she had received many marriage proposals.

*Electricity*

Eventually May chose and married Mr Wilber Ashford, a local sheep farmer and landowner. Wilber was a good honest man with a good income and not all pompous and stuffy and always had his top button undone on account of the wide girth of his neck, wrote May, and she admitted she didn't cover her arms even when she went outside. The climate suited May it meant her two children weren't, 'all buttoned up neither.'

May told Rose to cash in her life savings and come over to Australia; with all her experience in service she knew Rose would have no problem finding a husband. The eligible men outnumbered the women by at least twenty to one.

Good odds thought Miss Rose but I am needed here. A good job, wages, a roof over my head, my own room, she believed she could do a lot worse.

Lady Ellen Storrington was a modern lady for her years. She had a bathroom but didn't use it for bathing like the Americans. No she used it to develop her photographs, would you believe it! She slept in a four poster bed. Lord Storrington slept in the room adjacent to Lady Storrington. They were that wealthy they didn't have to sleep together! And there used to be a canopy above the bed but it had been taken away to make room for the hanging electric reading light.

Hansbury Manor was one of the first houses in Sussex to have electricity. When Lady Storrington saw it she wanted it. 'What do we need electricity for?' Lord Storrington had asked her but when Lady Storrington wanted something she normally got her own way. So electricity was fitted throughout.

After the lighting came the appliances. An electric iron. Miss Rose didn't get on with the new smart electric iron. The damn thing got hotter and hotter and she had ruined two of Lady Storrington's blouses with it. And it had taken her two months to pay back the damage out of her wages. 'An electric iron, who would think of such a thing?' Rose preferred to stick to her flat irons, 'if you don't mind,' she said to Tilly, the fourth housemaid.

Tilly agreed with Rose, 'I'm scared of the electricity.' She hadn't read Mary Shelley's novel, Frankenstein, but she had certainly heard of it. 'Devil's work,' said Tilly. Miss Rose smiled.

Two months previously Lady Storrington had arranged to have a week's trial with a new electric cleaning machine; a vacuum cleaner, a huge monster of an object. It had a motor and pump. It sucked up all the dirt effectively. The problem was it was so big and heavy that it took both the odd-job man and Tom the under-gardener to carry it up the family staircase. It was too big to go up the servant's staircase and a servant never makes work for other servants. So when the trial period was over Miss Rose and the other servants continued to clean the carpets the way it had always been done, either by taking them outside and beating them with a carpet beater or sweeping with damp tealeaves using a dustpan and brush and good old fashioned elbow grease.

So they were all surprised when on Monday morning they had another delivery. It looked to be a smaller contraption this time. Miss Rose had never seen Lady Storrington look more alive than when she unwrapped the new vacuum cleaner. Her ladyship positively glowed. The

*Electricity*

odd-job man plugged it into the light fitting on the wall and switched it on. All at once the new machine surged into life with a rattle and a roar as the vacuum cleaner sucked the dirt from the drawing room carpet.

Miss Rose stood and watched with amazement as Lady Ellen Storrington went back and forth with glee, cleaning the drawing room carpet. 'Do you know I am quite enjoying vacuuming, I think I shall finish the carpet myself.'

'Very well Ma'am,' Miss Rose dutifully replied. As she left the drawing room and made her way to the servant's hall Miss Rose had one of those moments of clarity as though she too had been charged with a high voltage of electricity that had switched the light on in her head. Electricity was the servant of tomorrow, electricity would do the jobs that she did today.

Three weeks later her letter arrived in Australia.

May announced cheerfully to her husband Wilber. 'My sister Rose is coming to live with us. I'm so happy.'

'Does she look like you?' Inquired May's brother in law, Arthur.

'A lot like me and a lot like herself,' laughed May.

'You can come and meet her when her ship arrives and carry her suitcases for me.'

'I look forward to it.' Arthur replied. He had very strong arms.

# Half-Listening

Karen Antoni

Sue and Dave sat opposite each other at Harry's cafe. They had finished their breakfast and were drinking their coffee. Sue was talking. Dave wasn't listening. They had been together for over eight years. He had been distracted by a spot behind his ear. And he'd got half listening down to a fine art. It wasn't because he wasn't interested in what she had to say, it was just that after a while he had become familiar with her voice patterns, the tone and, if he was honest, she did repeat herself so, if he missed it the first time round, he could always hear it again and often within the hour.

The museum was one of those subjects she talked about a lot. She worked there and talked about the sessions she took, 'Victorian Bygones, Preston Manor and the Ghost tours, the Royal Pavilion and the Prince Regent.' Although when she mentioned the Prince he found himself listening avidly especially as she had started referring to him as the Prince of Pleasure and talking about George IV in such a dreamy way that Dave had to remind himself that it was

*Half-Listening*

George IV and he had been dead for at least two hundred years.

Sue had started a writing course at Hove Library. She talked about this and her ideas for stories, poems and scripts. He often thought she would do better if she wrote them down instead of talking about them. Then he could listen properly when they were finished and he could give some constructive criticism. He thought he was good at that.

Dave located the spot behind his ear, applied enough pressure between his thumb and finger and bingo, it burst. He was just about to smell the white puss when he sensed Sue was coming to a close so he thought better of it and wiped it on his cardigan.

'So, I'm not sure how long we will be able to use it,' said Sue.

Dave felt a rush of panic as he ran through his mental list of appropriate responses but all he could come up with was, 'Why not?'

Sue sensed he hadn't been listening and replied impatiently. 'Because there's not enough people in the group,' she looked at him with a look that said I'm not giving anything away.

It was like a test, he knew the answer. What was it? No, not the museum, yes he knew it. 'The availability of the room in the library,' he blurted out.

'Hmm,' said Sue.

Dave felt pleased with himself. He loved Sue and would hate her to think of him as anything but attentive.

'I'm going into town. What are you doing this afternoon?' Asked Sue.

He had told her at least ten times that he would probably go to B&Q to get an insulated screwdriver. She never listened.

'OK and don't forget… the mushrooms for the Carbonara sauce,' Sue, reminded Dave.

They gave each other a quick peck goodbye.

On the way home just as Dave was about to walk past the shop he stopped. Onions, for the sauce, he thought feeling pleased with himself for remembering.

# Marriage Proposal?

Kay Beer

George knew she was his damsel in distress, an English rose needing to be saved, protected from the false knight's armoured horse powered truck.

Dairy farmer by day, George was asleep in his bed when Estelle knocked on his door, her car broken down.

Wanting to lay down his life for a chance to make her happy he invited her to use his telephone.

Proffering tea, a warm chair by the aga he wondered, could he win her heart?

An old knight at 59, past his prime, but if asked Estelle would have lain beneath the stars with him forever.

# Rainbows End

Kay Beer

Her dream life of living on the river was in tatters. Carol found herself sitting on the bulk head of the old empty barge wondering how it had all gone wrong. The departure of her husband, who couldn't cope with this massive restoration project, had shattered her vision of living a different way. Maybe the cracks had already been there in their relationship and she had been too busy papering over the fissures to see what was happening between them and she just kept papering over them hoping that the glue would keep them stuck together. Now all she owned was this heap of junk, a part built home for her and the two kids, but there was no time to feel sorry for herself she had to keep going, get the project back on track and finish it. This was their home. Gritting her teeth she looked at the barge, she had to complete the refit. Make it a home. There was no other choice. Going back home to live with her mum was out of the question, not with the kids in tow.

Undaunted at the vast job that lay ahead of her she took

her anger out on the hull of the barge, with each blow she repeated her mantra, 'Damn you, how dare you leave.' Muttering, 'why did you leave me alone?' Carol was determined beyond measure, somehow she held on and got the kids to school, cooked meals and worked as the unpaid navvy on the wreck they called their domicile. It was a permanent building site and funds were dwindling faster than she liked, the money slipped between her fingers like water, or could control as it consumed great vast chunks of cash faster than a sinking ship. Needing help of all sorts of trades people both professional and pure grunt, she was taciturn about approaching and asking strangers for support and she kept silent about letting on how tough life had become for her and the kids. Bravely or foolishly she ploughed on single handed, until she got to a point where she had no choice but to ask for help. She had taken books out from the library but accepted her limits, because she did not have the tools or the cash. This job wasn't one that she could tackle, she was capable of doing all the dirty heavy work but technical jobs like electrics and carpentry were out of her range.

Venturing out in to the boatyard that formed their community she began to talk to some of the boat owners to ask for advice and was genuinely surprised at their warmth and generosity. Only too pleased to give her a hand and help her out, she found another boat owner who was happy to complete her electrics. He offered her a favourable hourly rate if she in return would do some child minding for him, as his wife was giving him a hard time that they had no social life and his kids were about the same age as Carol's.

Understanding his predicament completely, Carol laughed loudly, she knew what having no social life felt like and was happy to help out seeing as he was about to save her life.

John had been openly shocked and surprised when he first saw the mess Carol and her kids were living around but slowly the barge progressed as he enlisted more support from other locals and told Carol that all she had to do was feed them in return for their labour. So weekends became more sociable as helpers arrived and getting jobs done with no cash changing hands was the biggest boost she could have had at this point in her project. Cooking up a storm she fed her willing army of workers who transformed the former hovel into her residence and ekeing out her limited reserves was paramount if she was to succeed in this madness called adventure. As the weeks flew by John came to like Carol hugely, she was a spunky woman who deserved better and he wondered how or why her husband had left, ditching her with the kids. It wasn't his usual game to interfere in people's lives but he felt she could benefit from some male company and he thought his mate Lawrence would be a good companion for her, Lawrence was a good guy, shy quiet and retiring who would benefit from her enthusiasm for life. Setting about match making was dangerous but John felt impelled to encourage these two to meet up and he hoped they would get on. Gingerly he began persuading Carol to think about asking Lawrence to lend a hand.

'Carol if you talk to Lawrence, he will be happy to do the carpentry that you need done to finish your kitchen.'

'Oh, why, where's Lawrence based?'

'Down the bottom of the boat yard, 'Class Act' turn left

at the end you will find him tucked away where the track terminates,' winking at her, adding, 'Take him a cup of tea.'

'Are you sure about this? She seemed hesitant to ask yet another person, an unknown guy for a favour, 'why would he help?'

'I've mentioned him to you,' grinning at her, winking again, knowingly. 'Told him how hard you've worked.'

Hesitantly Carol set off down the yard to find her carpenter. Entering his workshop she found a slim shortish guy with greying hair scraped back into a tight thin ponytail at the nape of his neck, wearing one ear ring and a bandana, a bright pink and white pattern. Walking in the air was pine scented and she breathed in deeply - she loved the smell of the fresh shaved wood - proffering her cup of tea.

'Hi... John sent me. I need to ask you... for your help, I'm Carol my boat is 'Rainbow's End.' Getting tongue tied she began to lose her nerve and started to stumble over her words it was harder enlisting his support than she had imagined or rehearsed. Out of practice and finding that Lawrence was painfully shy, with his arms folded firmly across his chest he nodded at the bench where Carol placed the cuppa. She wasn't the least bit sure he was pleased to see her.

'What do you need done?'

'Everything,' laughing nervously.

'Can you be more specific?' he asked pointedly.

'Fitted kitchen, panelling. I've got some drawings, just rough ideas, some basic sketches ... well outlines.'

'Well leave them with me and I'll see what I can do to help.'

Retracing her steps back to her barge she felt foolish and doubted she would hear from him in a hurry. She had not put forward a convincing request for anything. Hanging her head and ramming her hands deep into her jean pockets she felt forlorn.

John was packing up ready to go home. 'How'd it go?'

'Not well. I got tongue tied, and I didn't explain anything properly.'

'Lawrence is a good guy, he'll be fine, just wait and see. Besides I'll put a good word in for you.'

'Thanks John.'

'Bye.'

'Night.'

A few days later Carol, armed with another cup of tea, ventured out to see Lawrence. This time the encounter was a little easier, John was in the workshop so conversation was less stilted than her initial introduction. So the game continued and each time she took Lawrence a cup of tea their chats lasted longer, he grew easier more comfortable around her and unfolded his arms until Carol got brave enough to ask him to come on board her boat and have a look at her project. He was as shocked as John at the disarray that she and the kids lived around, how they had survived in the Heath Robinson set up appalled him. Like John he felt impelled to help her out. It was the least he could do.

Watching him work on her barge was fascinating, she loved to just sit and watch - which was probably unnerving for him - but his quiet resolute attitude grew on her, he was a true craftsman. Taking care over every joint and cut, ensuring that everything fitted perfectly, helped Carol to finally fall in love with her home after all the hardship she had endured.

The kids loved their new bedrooms, brightly coloured and based on a nautical theme, the cabin beds he made were perfect.

Over the summer months they spent time together and she worked hard around him finishing the barge off to a very high standard until finally one Tuesday early in September all the work was completed. It had been a long hard journey but worth every second, she had grown in so many ways. Carol had discovered new skills, grown in stature and made new friends, local people were impressed with her determination to make a go of things despite the odds, and it had turned around in a way that she could not have imagined nine months earlier. The community she lived among respected her drive and strength of mind because she had shown them she was a grafter and she'd developed a fantastic new support network returning favours where they were owed, offering to cook for anyone who wanted her help. Her reputation for making soup and hearty stews was well known locally because she had a knack of turning a few simple ingredients onto a satisfying tasty meal.

When her husband had left she had not really believed it would turn out this well.

Especially as, unexpectedly, once the work was done Lawrence told her he was going to miss working alongside her and seeing her every day. 'I've got used to you being around and making me cups of tea.'

Beaming at him she knew he was the one for her and bravely she slipped her hand into his, 'Let's go for a walk.'

With his defences down he didn't refuse and they set off for their initial late evening walk along the estuary, the first of many to come, hand in hand.

# Kissing the Pavement

Kay Beer

Samantha bit into her pasta, spicy pepper cappelletti. Steam escaped scalding the inside of her mouth. She spat. Then squealed. The offending half-chewed, mangled piece of pasta flew through the air and landed softly in the hollandaise sauce of her dates' Eggs Benedict. Samantha groaned, hung her head in her hands, and attempted to hide her shame, as she babbled helplessly, 'I'm so sorry.'

She heard him put down his knife and fork as she lifted her head and saw Joshua staring at her stony faced, unamused.

'Oh god... I'm sorry. How can I apologise for such,' she paused scrabbling for the correct wording, 'appalling behaviour?' Unable to stop herself, a torrent of garbled words poured out incoherent.

Samantha took immediate action calling the waiter over to their table. 'Please take this away.' She flapped her hand pointing at Joshua's meal and said. 'Bring a fresh plate, please.' She beamed at her favourite waiter. 'Thank you.'

'No. Don't bother,' came Joshua's stern reply. 'Cancel that meal.'

Samantha felt wretched.

'Let me make it up to you,' she pleaded. She wondered if batting her eyelids was appropriate game play. She had no idea how far to push her luck.

'I've gone right off the idea of eating.' He added sarcastically, 'Can't imagine why.'

Samantha grinned at him, she needed to make amends. 'Let's go for a drink? The Bear is just down the road.' She resisted touching his hand that lay flat on the table, giving him her best winning smile. 'The least I can do is buy you a drink.'

It was no good fretting. She prayed to the unseen goddesses because she wasn't sure if he was about to ditch her. Samantha couldn't blame him if he did. He was rather cute and she fancied getting to know him a little more intimately, given the right chance.

'Please,' she implored him. Joshua didn't look that receptive. She dipped her head, fluttered her eyelashes unabashed in his direction. Was it too late to play her self-assured feminine hand? She was painfully aware it had been an unpromising start to a first date.

Then she smiled, a big wide smile. That should clinch it she thought.

He relented, begrudgingly. 'Okay.'

But his tone didn't reassure her, even if Joshua had decided to give her a second chance.

They left the Café and walked down the High street side by side but not close. The street thronged with people rushing and bustling around. Saturday lunchtime was always busy.

Joshua balled up his hands and pushed them deep inside his coat pockets and wondered if she was worth bothering with, this particularly dippy female. He had been looking forward to meeting her. Her credentials on the dating website had looked promising. She had explained herself with ease, been funny and amusing when writing to him. Her emails were clear and concise. But she had not lived up to his expectations and if he was honest he was sorely disappointed.

Samantha tried to recover the situation. 'So if you weren't here where would you rather be?' she asked brightly. It was an opening gambit, well intentioned, if a little off key.

'New York,' he said.

'Wow, me too. I've never been, always wanted to go. It's top of my wish list alongside Las Vegas.'

'Really,' he was unimpressed.

'Yeah, but not until I've got my new patchwork velvet coat.'

'Huh!' He came up short, it was the oddest answer he'd heard as a reason for waiting to travel to one of the top cities in the world, one he hadn't anticipated nor expected because it simply made no sense. He smiled inwardly, it was ironic he thought. The randomness of her comment suited his newest companion to a tee. She was slightly off beat and this made him curious.

Joshua was about to respond with a witty cutting comment when the rim of Samantha's boot caught the uneven lip of the pavement.

She tripped and stumbled. She righted herself. Squealed.

Her arms flailed wildly, outstretched to balance her body. She stepped back off the twisted foot, slipped, skidded, lost her footing. Catapulted herself into the air.

Samantha sailed through the cold winter air a few inches above the pavement. She assumed a superwoman position, flying horizontally. She looked hilarious. Her hands outstretched as she landed heavily, unceremoniously sprawled across the pavement a few yards ahead of him.

His whole body wanted to catch the wave of convulsion and he wanted to burst out laughing but as she impacted the grey cement slabs he thought, *Ow* that had to hurt.

People stopped. Turned and came running in all directions offering her help. Stunned, Samantha could only hear a stampede of unseen shoes and boots. She felt vulnerable. There was little she could make out through tear glazed eyes as these heavily shod feet stomped towards her unprotected head.

Joshua knelt at her side dismissing offers of assistance from strangers in the crowd that quickly assembled into a large throng.

'It's okay,' he said out loud to reassure the encroaching gathered group, 'she's with me.' Concerned he asked, 'Samantha, are you okay?'

There was no response from her prone body.

He reacted quickly. Joshua knew what he was doing. He was a senior triage nurse at the local hospital. He thought it was lucky for Samantha he was still around.

'Back up, give her some space,' Joshua yelled firmly. He tucked down to her level and as he continued in earnest to assess her predicament. He saw large silent tears rolling down her cheek pooling on the cold pavement. He was grateful when the assembled group shuffled backwards a few feet.

'Samantha, I want you to stay still.' He pulled off his overcoat and spread it across her body, tucking it gently around her. 'Let me check you out.' He lifted her wrist carefully and, his eyes fixed on his watch, he checked her pulse. He monitored it. A strong regular rhythm it raced frenetically but that was scarcely surprising.

'Samantha, where does it hurt?' He sounded confident and in control.

'My pride,' she halted, 'I'm winded, that's all,' lying breathlessly.

'Let me be the judge of that,' he sounded brusque, business like.

She did not move, just attempted to nod her head. But it barely moved a fraction. Her cheek felt sore as it scrubbed the pavement.

'Stay down okay.' I'll check you all over. You're safer lying flat.'

'I'm okay. Honestly,' she said, trying to sound convincing. 'I can wriggle my fingers and toes. Look. See.' Her eyes darting furiously to and fro as if it made any real difference. 'You klutz', rattled around in her skull, crashing into a myriad of other equally self deprecating thoughts. She had no idea what to do next.

'Okay, that's good. There's no rush. You seem to be okay. I want you to sit up when you're ready.' He said.

She allowed a few moments to pass before rolling on to her side. As the world hoved into view she felt conspicuous, like an abandoned grey whale left on the beach to die, graceless and large. With the potentially fascinating spectacle over the small diminishing disinterested crowd dispersed.

Joshua noted that as she sat up she looked pale.

She placed her hands in her lap turned them over. Her palms were grazed. A thin layer of dirt embedded in to the soft flesh. They throbbed and stung almost as much as her bruised and dented ego. She had never anticipated kissing the pavement on her first date, well at least not while she was sober. Kissing her date was more along the lines of her overall plan.

Joshua squatted down next to her. 'You're lucky. Not a mark on you,' he grinned slyly at her, 'I was expecting at least two broken front teeth!'

She smirked then offered him a broad beaming grin, showing him her undamaged perfect pearly white teeth. Holding this false pose for just a few seconds made her ribcage object and rebel as it throbbed.

This wonderful smile lit up her face and Joshua could see she was being brave. He was impressed that she had listened and responded well to all his instructions.

He looked at her closely. 'You saved your face, how?'

'I have no idea.' She shrugged her shoulders. Her voice wavered, 'I haven't exactly made a great impression have I?'

A soft smile spread across his face as he responded sincerely, 'I promise you, you have made a lasting impression. One I will never forget.'

Samantha wrapped her arms around her torso, hugging her ribcage gently, trying to support her aching frame, laughing, she complained bitterly, 'ouch that hurts!' She begged him to stop. 'Don't make me laugh, please.' She wondered if she had bruises yet. She felt crushed. How could she tell him that her breasts ached? They had cushioned her impact, acted like car air bags. Her whole chest smarted. 'I think I'd better go home.'

'No I think we'd better get that drink. You're in shock. When you can stand we could go along to The Bear, it's not far,' he pointed along the street. 'Just a few doors…'

'Okay.' She nodded truly relieved that he hadn't taken flight leaving her alone to fend for herself.

He stood up. 'I think you should be okay walking now,' he said encouraging her to join him.

Ungraciously she twisted up on to all fours, wincing as her scuffed palms and bashed up knees bore the brunt of her weight. She felt like a class clown. The light headed sensation she experienced was a little unnerving, especially as she couldn't be woozy yet, she hadn't drunk any alcohol.

Joshua offered her his arm. He looked serious. She liked the sensation that he cared, but fretted that as he watched her clamber to her feet and stand upright he was anticipating her to lose her footing again. Limply she smiled and accepted his gracious offer, trying to paste on a happy face to mask her trampled pride.

Arm in arm they walked at an unusually slow pace. Her knees complained, creaked, she almost shuffled as they stiffened up. Samantha was tempted to lean into his body. She liked the feeling of her arm being tucked beneath his and wanted to snuggle in close.

'Southern Comfort, please, no ice,' she asked. Gingerly she sat down on the nearest free seat in the pub. Slugging back her drink in one hit, it barely touched the sides.

Joshua looked on, 'Another one?'

'Yes please… thank you.'

As he stood at the bar he watched her unnoticed as she inspected her knees. A few heads at the bar checked her out. He saw what they saw. A pretty woman. Slightly kooky. Nice figure. Slender with gentle curves. Enough to get hold of.

Looking down at her out stretched knees she surveyed the damage. Her new trousers were ruined, they had melted. The holes revealed her knee caps where her skin had broken and bled. Small red dried blood stains encrusted, dirty with grit and dust.

'Roll up your trousers,' he said.

'No,' she protested. 'Really it's okay. You've done enough.'

'That's a 'no' then.' Raising one eyebrow. 'Roll them up,' he demanded, kneeling down in front of her.

Samantha had a good looking guy go down on his knees at her feet. Magical fleeting thoughts of a man proposing marriage flew though her mind's eye. A snivel of desire stuck in her throat. She coughed. This charade was not lost on her for one moment, she flinched.

Oh the agony. The shame of it. She had not shaved her legs. Deliberately, to stop herself from jumping into bed on a first date with a new bloke, just in case this possibility arose. She vaguely remembered thinking how it seemed a great idea earlier this morning in the shower. Now she felt dim and silly. Whimpering, she did as she was bid. It took all her effort to lean forward and bend, to fold at her midriff, to wind up her trouser legs. Folding at her waist almost left her out of breath.

Joshua didn't seem to notice her unsightly winter stubble, dabbing her grazed knees gently with neat alcohol, from her glass, with a clean handkerchief. It stung her broken skin.

'Ouch,' she remonstrated, sucking in the air with each dab, at the same time as being dead impressed that he carried a clean ironed hanky. Not something you saw every day, she thought.

'Stop whinging, big softie.' He unwrapped and with care he positioned the Mr Men plasters across the biggest scrapes carefully. Applying them gently he ensured that they were securely stuck.

'Aren't you going to kiss them better,' she asked cheekily, finding her sense of humour at last.

'I'm not your mother.' Looking up at her from under long glorious eyelashes, she considered far too lush for any young man.

'Shame,' she replied, beaming at him.

Laughing with her, seeing her mascara run down the side of her cheek that had lay on the pavement, she was dishevelled, but looking into her eyes he saw humour. Her tousled blond hair piled heavily on one side needed to be brushed, smoothed back into place. She hadn't seemed to have noticed so he resisted the urge to place it where he thought it ought to go. He was surprised he was enjoying himself. Despite their date having gone off script he was warming to her quirkiness.

What was left of her second glass of Southern Comfort

she sipped more slowly but as she raised her glass her arm shook unsteadily, almost out of her control.

'I think it's about time I took you home, okay. I need to make sure you're good,' he offered, 'we'll get a taxi.'

Raising her glass, she looked directly at him. 'A toast,' she beamed.

He looked at her hesitantly.

'New York,' she said.

As they chinked their glasses, 'New York,' looking at her a little confused, almost dreading her answer, but then maybe that was part of her attraction. She kept him guessing as he had no idea what was coming next. 'Why do you need a patchwork velvet coat?'

# Poisonous Thoughts

Kay Beer

Bruce loved Mary. He idolised his wife. Nothing made him happier than feeling the warmth of her naked skin next to his. Married for almost forty years he was looking forward to their retirement. No big plans just domesticity and togetherness. He wanted nothing more than to spend time with his beloved.

Mary missed her sons. She wished her boys lived closer to home because they had both flown the nest after university. Scott had travelled the globe and settled in Vancouver. Mary had accepted this decision but she was not happy. Eighteen months later Alexander had married an Australian lass and lived in Adelaide. Mary was devastated and fretted at the loss of both sons to distant continents. 'When will we see our grandchildren?' she wailed to her husband.

'We'll find a way I promise.' He wasn't sure how they would afford it but he could find a solution.

On his daily commute to work he passed an old Victorian

villa and a pair of terraced cottages put up for sale. It was perfect. Ideal for the two of them. They bought one half of the pair and downsized. Moving in to this cosy workman's cottage completed Bruce's retirement dream. The cottage was set back from the road with a long front garden. He intended to dig this over and grow soft fruits and delicate vegetables. Inside was homely but it needed a fresh coat of paint. A new bathroom suite was put in by a professional team to update this new home. Outside the back garden went on forever, down the bottom corner, close to the stream, he built a summerhouse for afternoon tea.

Mary adored the summerhouse. An ideal spot to hide, escape to with a good book and relax.

Bruce's final retirement day drew closer. He anticipated Mary would retire at around the same time, it was what they had agreed.

Mary arrived home from work and stopping at the gate she watched her husband digging over the front garden. Leaning on the picket fence she watched his body move effortlessly. She knew he loved his garden.

'Dinner will be on the table in half an hour,' she smiled at him.

'Okay,' he nodded and resumed turning heavy clods of earth over to break into smaller clumps. Physical work that kept him fit.

Over dinner Bruce suggested that they book a week away in Devon. 'I thought we would go somewhere nice to celebrate my retirement,' smiling genially at his wife.

'When?' Mary clarified as she cleared the table of dishes.

'June seventh.'

*Poisonous Thoughts*

'I'll see if I can get time off work,' Mary replied nonchalantly.

'Pardon,' Bruce looked taken aback, 'you're not stopping work too?' He looked perplexed.

This was a disagreement Mary had wanted to avoid but she wasn't going to able to side step this issue now, she took a deep breath, 'No.'

'But, we agreed,' he protested.

'I know,' she looked out of the kitchen window, 'I can't,' she said forcefully, leaning heavily against the sink.

'Why can't you?' he demanded.

'I need the money.'

'No, we don't need your money, we're going to be fine.'

'No we're not.'

'Yes we are.'

'But how will I visit the boys?'

Bruce was stunned.

'How are we going to afford flights every year?' She looked at him, pleading with him to try to see her point of view.

'We agreed we'd visit them every couple of years.'

'That was before the grandchildren were born.' Mary sounded determined. 'I want to see my granddaughters grow up, every couple of years won't do!'

Bruce left the kitchen and walked out to the garden, he took his anger out on the earth. Digging furiously. Venting his anger.

Mary felt uncomfortable letting Bruce down, there had been no easy way to tell him that she had changed her mind. She reckoned he would come round, eventually, and understand her reasoning.

Bruce retired. Being home all day alone wasn't quite how he'd imagined things would work out. He missed Mary's company. He felt incomplete.

As a concession Mary reduced her hours and came home earlier each day with Wednesday afternoons off. It helped temporarily to ease their disagreement in the short term. The summer passed quietly as they settled into their new routines enjoying the warm evenings with a glass of wine as the sun set over their newly planted rose garden. On warm evenings the garden was scented and fragrant, a real joy to both of them. Bruce kept busy working the allotment, planning the vegetable calendar for the front and back gardens and doing all the odd jobs around the house.

Time flew by.

Their week's holiday in Devon, during late September, was a huge success, a second honeymoon. They found their romantic tryst bought them closer together. And as October arrived Mary broached the subject of going to Adelaide. 'I thought I'd book tickets for us to fly out on Boxing Day, a sort of Christmas present for both of us,' she smiled at him, her best winning smile.

Bruce hesitated, 'It's a very long way to fly.'

'I know but it will be an adventure.'

'I'm not sure.' It was bad enough flying two hours to Spain. Bruce hated flying so the idea of flying for twenty four hours or more in one stretch terrified him.

'We'd get to see Millie,' hoping to persuade him, 'she'll be eight months old.'

Trying to be magnanimous, 'Why don't you go on your own?'

'What?' She quizzed him closely, 'Don't you want to see Millie?'

'It's not like that,' he hung his head in shame…

Mary let this conversation drop, she didn't want an argument. She would try to change his mind over the coming weeks.

Mary booked her ticket and she assumed he would change his mind before she flew. He didn't. Christmas day dinner was a very quiet affair, the two of them and a couple of long distance phone calls to the boys.

Eager to go, she had been packed ready to fly for a fortnight. Bruce was subdued. Mary became excited. He would drive her to the airport and watch her fly away filled with fear. What if she never came back?

Mary hugged Bruce goodnight, 'I'll be back before you've missed me,' she whispered.

There was no response. He rolled over in bed and ignored her.

'I've put all your favourite dinners in the freezer. You just have to reheat them.'

Holding her husband fast, she wondered how bad he'd be in the morning at the airport. It was going to be tough saying goodbye.

'Can't I get you to change your mind?' she waited for his response. 'We could book you a ticket at the airport?'

How she wished he had changed his mind but all her fun and flirtatious efforts to persuade him had failed.

Bruce dropped her at departures, he stiffened when she hugged him.

'I love you,' she said, 'be back twenty fourth.' Holding

back her emotions she was determined not to cry at the departure gate. She stood, turned, smiled and waved. It nearly broke her heart looking at him, he looked so dejected.

Bruce fled the airport, back to the safety of his allotment. January was the coldest longest, darkest month of his life. Snow lay nine inches thick across his garden and allotment for more than eight days. Pacing up and down at home with no idea how to fill those short dark winter days, he was housebound like a demented shabby old lion he patrolled the boundaries and waited. He stopped ringing Mary, he hated hearing her voice because it was too distant. It made him maudlin. He avoided answering the phone when it rang. Praying she would leave a message on the answer phone that he could play back over and over. Hearing her voice made him feel calm when he could hit replay.

Mary came home tanned, beautiful and animated. Sharing all her many photographs and tales of Millie. How tall she was, her efforts to walk and the first sounds that everyone tried to make sense of. He listened glad to hear her dulcet tone. Bruce breathed again.

A few weeks passed, and their old routines resumed. Bruce was feeling settled, happier than during her absence. 'Shall we see Scott at Easter?' She asked over breakfast early one beautiful spring morning.

Wounded, he hid his fear. 'But you've just got back,' he lamented.

'I know,' she walked across to him, stroked his arm, 'but little Annie will be almost a year old and Scott can't afford to fly all three of them home to visit us. So how about it?' She thought she had left enough time for him to get over her trip to Adelaide. 'Besides its closer that Australia?' She reasoned. 'Not quite so far to fly. What do you think?' Mary dearly wanted him to go with her on this next trip. Smiling at him she waited.

Canada was no closer than Australia, as far as Bruce was concerned. Mary made it sound easy but it wasn't that simple. He stomped off out to his potting shed to quietly vent his spleen. How could she do this to him so soon? Picking up the rhododendron plant feed to make up a solution, he spotted the rat poison out of the corner of his eye.

In an instance he saw the answer to his prayers. He picked up the packet and read the instructions. If he could just incapacitate her enough, clip her wings, so to speak. Make her more dependent on him. He knew care would be required. He could tend to her needs like his allotment. Hopefully he could care for her full time, show her how much he loved and needed and wanted her. She was the only person he wanted to spend time with. He needed her to need him more.

Heading back indoors, he flicked the switch and put on the kettle, 'Tea darling?'

# Left versus Right

Kay Beer

Polly had not expected to bump into Adam Cox at the local mini supermarket. It was an unanticipated pleasure on that dull damp Saturday afternoon. Did she look okay? She wondered. She felt self-conscious and how she wished she had washed her hair earlier that morning! If only she had made a little more of an effort to get dressed up, instead of wearing her much-loved ripped jeans and favourite old t-shirt.

As he put down his shopping basket, he beamed at her.

'It's been ages.' He placed his hand on her arm. 'Tell me everything, all the juicy bits…'

His broad grin made her go mushy, deep down inside.

She had last seen him ten years ago at a human resources meeting but over the years they had lost touch because he worked abroad. Adam still looked the same to her. A tall guy, but his blond hair had turned silver, which made him look distinguished, more handsome and quite striking in her opinion. Polly did her best not to gush, he looked so dreamy.

## Left Versus Right

They talked animatedly as old familiar friends, blocking the narrow aisle oblivious to all manner of confusion and congestion that they caused their fellow shoppers. She was enjoying his relaxed easy chatter, which came to an abrupt change.

Adam hurriedly explained: 'I must go, my father's in hospital and patient visiting started twenty minutes ago.' He looked at his watch. 'Sorry, but I've got to dash.'

Then he surprised her. 'Join me for lunch next weekend?' He beamed at her as he left, no longer able to stand still and wait to hear her response.

'Okay.' Polly agreed speedily. She smiled to herself, satisfied. Wrapped up in a myriad of thoughts about how lucky she felt to have bumped into him after so long an absence she promptly forgot to buy the vital ingredients required for her supper.

During the week she sent up a silent pray that the weather would be kind to her and be good for the following weekend. It always cheered her up if the sun shone. But if it was inclement she'd have a good excuse to suggest a country pub with a cosy atmosphere.

When she got home from work she hit the answering machine button and stood stock still as Adam's voice pierced the silence and filled the hallway. 'Hi Polly. About Sunday, would you mind meeting me at my house, say midday? Hope this is okay with you, looking forward to seeing you. Bye.' He left her his address and number.

The answering machine fell silent. Polly leapt with joy, hugged her arms around her body, she danced around her flat. Then she raced upstairs to her attic bedroom. She felt a great need to review her wardrobe, to work out what she could wear. She wanted to look sexy. Better still drop dead gorgeous.

Sunday morning dawned. A thin pale blue sky, strung with a paper trail of white wispy clouds threaded in all directions had been painted just for her. She was happy and in a great mood as she drove to his house. She was surprised at how easy it was to find. It clung to the steep incline and from his home she could see panoramic views across the valley.

Polly took in a breath and started to climb the steep flight of steps up to his front door. She admired the view, gave herself time to regain her composure before she rang the bell.

As he opened the door Adam beamed at her. 'Morning.'

Standing below him on the front step she realised how tall he was, at six foot four inches, he towered over her and he made Polly feel protected if not a little self conscious. And short. She felt shorter than usual despite wearing her highest heels.

As he swooped down to peck her on the cheek she caught the scent of his aftershave. It was heaven. She laughed, trying to cover her nervousness at his casual and carefree manner because he caught her off guard. He threw on his leather jacket and picked up his house key. He was ready to go.

She looked hard at the man in front of her. He was thinner than she had remembered and this worried her and then she wondered if she might cut herself on the sharp edges. But he had taken care to dress, casual but smart. His

*Left Versus Right*

jeans emphasised his long legs and his jacket masked his lack of a backside.

As they left the house Polly offered to drive which Adam seemed happy to accept but of course she had no idea how foolish a notion this was.

Unaccustomed to his closeness, with Adam as her passenger, Polly was gripped by a flurry of nerves that made her become more flustered as she drove. All her practical ability vacated her and everything went to hell in a hand basket.

Adam gave clear concise directions which Polly's brain attempted to compute.

'Next right,' was clear enough.

Polly swung the steering wheel and hooked a left.

Adam kept calm and asked, 'could you turn right at the next junction, please?'

Polly dutifully obliged by taking the next left. She had no concept that she was driving him in the wrong direction.

'Typical woman driver,' he said jovially, 'so, you don't know your right from your left?' laughing at her, but not expecting an answer.

Being hopelessly flummoxed Polly threw him a sideways glance. 'Am I going the wrong way?' she asked.

'Yes.'

'Oh.' She did her best not to blush.

They laughed together at their odd predicament.

'Ahead, next junction, turn right, please…'

Polly failed. Her car turned left. She smiled, certain she had followed his instruction to the letter.

Adam laughed out loud, hung his head in his hands as

he brushed away casual tears, 'Holy cow,' was all he could say as he hooted genially.

At the next junction she turned left of her own accord.

There had been no further instruction offered from her bemused passenger.

'Do you think that there is any chance that you could at some point turn right please, and head in the general direction of the coast? Towards the sea, instead of away from it?' as he raised his eyebrows and looked over the top of his sunglasses.

Polly realized he sounded somewhat exasperated and perhaps driving her date round the bend was not the best way to secure a second date however endearing or charming this peculiar trait of hers was, not know her left from her right.

As they approached the next crossroads Adam changed tactics. 'Follow that taxi cab,' he pointed to the one ahead them. It seemed such a simple request. But life is not simple and in the twenty seconds that it took for her car to reach the intersection two more taxis turned up from different directions at the appointed junction.

Together they collapsed into a heap of giggles, faced by three taxis she had no hope of turning in the desired direction.

He threw a long arm across her body and he yelled 'That way.'

'Oh. Right, okay.'

'Halleluiah. Yes. Right…at last, thank you.'

The remainder of their short journey passed without incident and finally they arrived at the beach.

Polly redeemed herself slightly when she parallel parked in a proficient manner close to the kerb in a tight spot.

He was impressed, she can park, he thought, and then he laughed at himself. And she can do something without instruction!

They ambled off along the promenade to find a beach front restaurant.

They sat in the bright sunshine on a clear May-day to eat lunch by the sea. It was a novel experience but the table was a tad too close to the front.

Polly felt uncomfortable. The walkway teemed with pedestrians who strolled hither and thither enjoying this unexpectedly balmy afternoon. It was crammed.

'When do you next fly to Holland?' She asked.

'Not sure, this damn ash cloud is causing all sorts of problems. My flight's been cancelled, again.'

'Of course, that reminds me. I must buy powdered milk.'

Adam stopped eating, looked at her, puzzled by her comment.

But unperturbed she continued to eat her meal.

He watched, waited for an explanation. And exactly how is the ash cloud connected to powdered milk? He wondered.

Her face changed from relaxed and happy to outright shock. Polly dropped her knife and fork. The cutlery fell clattering on to her plate.

'Oh shit.' she exclaimed. Then she gulped nosily as she wished she could concertina down and hide beneath the table.

Adam looked mystified.

'My parents,' she squeaked as her dad waved to her whilst he nudged his wife, drawing his wife's attention to their daughter seated ahead of them.

'Hello,' her voice was flat and then sunk to a brooding tone.

'Hello darling,' her dad smiled at her.

Reluctantly, Polly introduced him to the couple, 'Mum, dad, meet Adam.'

Her heart pounded, her palms sweated, and her head was fit to burst. She wanted to scream with passion, Go away, mum. Not now!

Directed straight at her father, Polly's eyes blazed. What are you two doing here? She flashed her message as she pleaded with him to take her mother somewhere else, far away from here, when she heard Adam say.

'Would you like to join us for coffee? Please do.'

Polly nearly choked. How could he? God, she wanted to kick him in the shins, this was preposterous! How dare he? Somehow she resisted the urge to kick because she thought, can a datee kick her date on a first date? No. Don't be ludicrous, her internal voice yelled back.

Luckily her father declined Adam's generous offer and started to steer his wife by the elbow away from the couple, sensing his daughter's discomfort at their unplanned meeting.

'Shit, shit, shit' Polly muttered under her breath and as she glanced up she saw a delicious smile sweep across Adam's face. 'That was fun,' he said, 'watching you squirm, I wouldn't have missed it for the world.'

'You, you …' the word 'bastard,' died in her mouth as he lent forward and kissed her.

Her lips parted. His warm moist kiss consumed her, made her forget everything. She didn't want this kiss to end. He tasted so good, of raspberries and cream and she wished it was the first of many more luscious kisses.

# A Master of the Universe and a Humble Porky Pie

Liv Singh

Life was good. I had a warehouse apartment overlooking the River Thames, just along from Tower Bridge, and with my bonus last year I bought a rhiad in the old city of Marrakesh that I flew over to every other weekend.

Then the banks collapsed and credit crunched. Not that it threatens me. I'm an oil trader and everyone needs oil. But in the past six months even oil's been hit. When oil was at a hundred dollars a barrel my commission was good but once it slumped back to sixty you don't have to be a rocket scientist to work out my commission plummeted with it. I was used to earning big bucks on my deals and now I have to chase every lead out there to make even half the money I was bringing in last year.

On a normal market I wouldn't have bothered with the likes of old MacIntosh but case needs. The problem with old Maccy is he flaps around. He's too lily livered and can't take a decision until it's too late and the business has gone

*A Master of the Universe and a Humble Porky Pie*

elsewhere. That's why I have to encourage him to bite the bullet and make up his mind or he'd never do any business for his company.

I make no bones about it – I've had a bad month. It's a tough market to trade in. Even Bonners, the best trader on the desk, has fallen below his average for the year. So when Maccy boy came to me with his two hundred thousand tonnes of crude oil from Banda Abbas I knew I'd have to sweet talk him into a deal this side of the weekend or I'd miss getting any money into this quarter's figures.

It was only a little white lie when I told him the price was weakening and a deal had already been done below the price I was offering him and this was his last chance to take it. We concluded the contract just before close of business on Friday night.

When I told him to sell how was I to know that over the weekend the Americans were going to blockade the Straits of Hormuz to all shipping in or out. The markets went wild and the price of oil doubled within minutes of the announcement.

On Monday morning Mac was on the line to me spluttering with rage that I'd deliberately set him up and that he was going to sue my firm for gross professional negligence, misappropriation of funds and whatever else the lawyers could come up with. Obviously I told him my advice was given in all good faith. Markets can turn on the spin of a coin. He knows that as well as I. He's worked in the business long enough.

Well, later that day word went out that Mac was sacked. It's been common knowledge for ages that his firm had been looking for a way of getting rid of him without paying any redundancy. Poor old Mac – he's past his best.

I did feel sorry for the old boy when I heard on the grapevine that his daughter's got skin cancer. Apparently he's having to use his pension now to pay for her treatment in the USA.

It's a tough old world.

# After the Revolution

Liv Singh

Kim Fuller walked briskly across Trafalgar Square and stopped in front of Nelson's Column. She smiled broadly. She liked the way that Peter Mandleson had been paired up with David Cameron to clean the pigeon droppings off the stone plinth.

'Hey Pete, you've missed a bit,' she called playfully.

Peter's head was down and he scrubbed furiously at the stone. His face was red and his limp gray hair stuck to his sweaty forehead. David Cameron had pushed the sleeves of his pink Community Service jerkin up over his elbows. His eyes looked glazed and confused.

It had been this way ever since the Night of the Revolution in early June. The Old Elite, known generally as the OEs, had been rounded up and held at Buckingham Palace before being transferred to Wormwood Scrubs. The People's Revolutionary Party leaders had announced the Community Service Orders a week later. Anyone over the age of sixty five was excused service much to the relief of the

Queen and Prince Philip who were sent to a nursing home in Barnet. Sir Fred Goodwin, a mere fifty two year old, was one of the first to be put on road sweeping duty outside No.10 Downing Street. A huge crowd gathered to support him in his new work.

Kim felt there was something wholly uplifting in seeing ex-bankers and politicians welding brooms for the good of the nation. They were truly cleaning up British society as indeed they always had done, she mused, in one way or another.

The people she passed, as she continued on her way along Whitehall, all seemed to have a skip in their step and smiled readily back at her. Never in her life had Kim seen so many happy people.

A bill board for the Evening Standard proclaimed, 'Election Night Fever for the New Queen.' One of the first acts of the PRP had been to set up an election for a new, annual Queen. The contestants Joanna Lumley, Judi Dench and Glenda Jackson were unexpectedly beaten by the young upstart Kirsten O'Brien, the children's television presenter. The PRP had clearly given children the vote to good effect.

Tony Benn, Leader-in-Chief of the PRP, had won the support of the army by requisitioning the Royal Palaces as future homes for the disbanded military forces. Once the Generals had signed the Revolutionary Military Pact they were bundled off to Wormwood Scrubs to join the rest of the OEs. Many of the OEs were proving very useful in their new roles. Tony Blair was placed as a carer in the Military Hospice for War Casualties. He worked on the Iraq Ward and was well liked by all accounts. Quite a number of OEs had been given work in the MacPRP fast food restaurants. Kim had been served her Big Rev with chips only the evening before by ex-Major General Mike Jackson. He looked quite fetching, she thought, in his pink cap and overalls.

The budget looked much healthier without the military expenditure and the costs of maintaining a monarchy and their extended family, so much so in fact that there was more money for education and health. Housing had improved too when the second homes of the OEs were shared out amongst the homeless masses.

There were of course those who carped about the new order. Damien Hirst was one, who was none too pleased when the price of his art installations fell to an all time low. His patron, Mr Saatchi, regrettably for him, no longer had a disposable income of millions to spend on such frivolities. He found his time was valuably spent painting the walls of a comprehensive school in St John's Wood.

Kim arrived at her office. She found that her years as a cashier at the Nat West on Finchley High Street helped no end in her new role at No.11 Downing Street.

# No Fixed Abode

Liv Singh

Empty pockets, cold roofless bed,
Lost, I cannot find my way
Right, left, backward, forward
It all looks the same.

Adrift in space, no gravity to hold
A child screams
Panic grips
Fall, fall, fall.

The safety rope of hope
Lays severed on the floor
Whilst all around the stench of Alright Jack's
Soiled blanket of suffocating air.

# In the Secretary's Words

Liv Singh

I hate this boring job, it's doing my head in. I sit here staring at a screen all day arranging meetings for managers who barely acknowledge my existence. There are other aspects to the work of course, like making the tea. Where, I'd like to know, in the job description does it say 'make the tea?' Why can't they make it themselves? It adds to their feeling of self importance to have lackeys like me doing the menial stuff for them. The history books tell us that domestic servants disappeared after the First World War but what they don't say is that they've reappeared in the form of secretaries in the office world.

Yes, I'm angry and it's that feeling of resentment that got me into the trouble I'm now in.

I was typing yet another report full of words that either said nothing or hid what little meaning they had. It had long been a belief of mine that no one actually read all the papers that were attached to the agendas for the never ending meetings the managers went to. Acres of beautiful air cleansing forests had lost their lives for reports nobody read but the writer. Would anyone notice if I added a few words of my own deep in the inner depths of, 'The Strategic Planning Process'? It was only a few words, *'of all the pointless drivel, this takes the biscuit.'* It seemed to fit in quite well at the end of a paragraph on the need for blue sky thinking, out of the box, to fully engage with stakeholders and customers alike. The usual crap management speak we've all become familiar with.

Of course I regretted it as soon as the Board papers were sent out. What was I thinking? I needed the money the job gave me. I'm a wage-slave like everyone else in the country. Some know it, some don't. I got a sick feeling in my stomach when I thought about what I'd done. Whenever the Director glanced my way I felt guilty and put my head down and typed aimlessly. On the day of the Board meeting the sweat trickled down my armpit as I watched the directors' sweep into the boardroom.

But I got away with it. No one said a thing about my addition to the report. I got a thrill out of not being caught and it emboldened me to have another go.

My second excursion into print was the Equality and Diversity Quarterly Report. Its author, Emilia Ranson, is about four foot eleven and lives up to her nickname, 'the poison dwarf.' She gave me the inspiration for my next effort, *'never trust short people.'* I placed it in a particularly dense section about two thirds of the way through.

This time the adrenalin got pumping after I printed off the reports and added them to the rest of the treasury tagged wad of papers. It gave me a buzz as I furtively watched the faces of the directors who passed my desk. I thought I was really in for it when Amanda Pickford, the Human Resources Director, bore down upon me with a face like thunder. I looked at the screen in front of me and began tapping furiously at the keyboard.

'Debbie, have you printed off the agenda for this afternoon's Health Overview Scrutiny Committee meeting?'

'Sorry Amanda, the printer wasn't working yesterday afternoon and I forgot to do it this morning,' I trailed off weakly.

'Well perhaps you might find time to do it now,' she said, adding as an afterthought, 'Please.'

Amanda always sounded annoyed and had a permanently peevish look that did nothing to improve her face which looked like a stale donut.

'Yes,' I answered. I have this way of acting like a subservient moron when I'm in the office. I feel it's what the management expect of me and I like to please whenever it's in my power to do so.

After that second time it became an obsession with me. I took great care to select the right document and the most appropriate place to put my little treasures. Too close to the beginning or in the final paragraph and it was in danger of being spotted.

One of my favourites was in the Risk Analysis Report, *'martin webber picks his nose.'* I typed it all in lower case so his name wouldn't stick out. And he does too. I've seen him in his office, when he thinks no one is watching, with his finger up his nose.

I reckon if I had stuck to the reports no one would ever

have noticed but I got a bit too carried away with the thrill of getting one over on the professionals. In the minutes of the senior managers' meeting I put, '*ER said MW is a shyster. All agreed.*' Funny thing was it wasn't spotted immediately. I thought I'd got away with it again. Then one morning, months later, there was a flurry of directors in and out of the chief executive's office. I thought there must have been a major incident alert, a derailed train or a terrorist bomb in the shopping centre until Sandra, the chief executive's personal assistant, came mincing up to my desk in her high heeled shoes.

In a hushed whisper she said, 'The chief executive would like to see all the secretaries separately for a short interview. Someone has tampered with the minutes of a meeting. It's a very serious matter,' she added in her sing song Welsh accent.

I sat waiting for my turn to go in cursing the stupidity of my actions. Liz Thomas came out looking like a frightened rabbit but then again she usually looks that way. Should I just leave there and then and not go back? Get in first with the resignation before you have to suffer the ignominy of the boot like all those MPs always seem to do when they're caught out.

'Debbie, if you'd like to step in, the chief executive's ready for you now.' Was it my imagination or was there a menacing tone in Sandra's voice?

The interview with Mr Simpkins, the chief executive, although gruelling turned out to be not as bad as I'd feared. The backs of my legs stuck to the plastic of the seat and my skirt kept riding up my thighs, try as I did to pull it back down again. I don't think he believed my denial of all knowledge in the matter but when I told him Emilia Ranson did her own minutes and we secretaries only topped and tailed them I noticed a change come over him. His eyes which had seemed trapped in the cleft of my breasts came up to meet mine. 'Really,' he said and raised his eyebrows.

Later I discovered that Emilia, who I'd been told was off work with a urinary tract infection, was in fact on long term sick leave for stress. Sandra told me she'd found a drawer full of rotten fruit in Emilia's desk and a filing cabinet stuffed with unopened post and old copies of 'Heat' magazine.

'She's off her trolley, poor ducks. She won't be coming back to work. They've come to an arrangement with her.' Then she added, 'No action will be taken on the minutes.'

I nodded sympathetically and bit my lower lip to prevent the smile I could feel inside from spreading across my face.

# The Yard

Liv Singh

Suzie Chandler loved to plant out her carefully grown sunflower seedlings in early May and watch them grow all summer long until they poked their big, round, upturned faces over the high red brick wall at the bottom of her garden. By August she'd have a row of eight foot tall yellow headed guards turning their faces this way and that in a graceful arc from east to west, from morning to night, surveying the realm of her garden, and by late summer that of the garden beyond the wall.

Even a sixteen by sixteen foot backyard can take on the quality of a realm in the poorer parts of London. It is the only piece of the outside world to stand and feel the air, to throw back your head and admire the umbrella of the sky above.

Suzie remembered the first time she'd come to see the house with the estate agent. He'd taken her from room to room enthusiastically pointing out all the features and to Suzie, who at the time had been living in a tiny one bedroomed flat in Bloomsbury, it seemed like a rabbit warren palace, with all the little rooms stacked neatly one on top of another. She'd already made up her mind to buy it before she walked into the backyard.

It stopped her in her tracks. The buildings of the street behind loomed up in an unwanted threatening intimacy, blocking out the sky. It felt as if a pair of giant hands had pushed the two rows of terraced houses closer together. Suzie could hear the clatter of pots and pans in the kitchen of the house behind the garden wall as if she were standing in the same room as the unseen people. The smell of burnt food hit her nostrils.

But Suzie had a shrewd business head. So what if the house had a backyard the size of a postage stamp? It had four bedrooms and if she ever lost her job she'd let three of them out to pay the mortgage. Anyway, she reasoned, for most of the year the weather was so bad she wouldn't want to go into the garden.

Suzie's friends weren't so sure about her move to Hackney.

'Won't you feel afraid living there? It's not like Bloomsbury, you know. They don't call it "murder mile" for nothing darling.'

'It's an investment, plus, for little more than the price of my pad on Woburn Place it's got loads of rooms and character too. It's got the original stripped floorboards, cast iron fireplaces, shutters at the windows – it's a dream. And, more to the point, the estate agent reckons it'll increase in value by fifty percent by the time of the 2012 Olympics. I'll be quid's in.'

And so her fate was sealed.

During the first year she moved into the house she had a new kitchen and bathroom fitted by some young Polish builders recommended by one of the other junior partners of the law firm she worked for. Suzie was particularly pleased with the white, cast iron, roll top bath complete with claw feet that she'd hunted down in a salvage yard in Essex. Renovation works complete, she held regular dinner parties for her friends who came and admired the spaciousness of her new abode.

It was in that first spring that she began a makeover of the backyard. She placed large, terracotta pots of bamboo along each side wall and in the flower bed which ran along the back wall she planted out sunflowers for the first time. A chiminea and a small, white wrought iron, cafe style table and chairs completed the new look garden. Suzie was pleased with the final result.

First one family then another moved into the house beyond the wall. A soft plastic ball would sail over the wall into her garden from time to time. Suzie liked to think she was a tolerant sort of person and she cheerfully threw the balls back. It has to be said that on some occasions she felt less cheerful than on others, like the time a ball landed on one of her cherished cherry tomato plants, breaking the stems and crushing the fruit.

For a long passage of time no projectile objects came across from the land beyond. Two youngish men moved into the house and their pastimes did not include kicking plastic balls over the garden wall. Indeed Suzie noticed when she peeked from her upstairs windows that they were a fastidiously neat and tidy couple, at least in the parts of the house on view to her prying eyes. She imagined that the yard was just as tidy and clear of clutter, although she couldn't actually see it apart from a tiny sliver by the kitchen door.

The first Suzie knew of the change of occupants was when she found a dirty nappy on her bistro table. It had burst open and flies were swarming over the revealed contents. She could hear the noise of squabbling children in the yard behind the wall interspersed with the guttural oaths of their parents telling them to be quiet. It was the start of a new era in Suzie's life.

After the nappy episode came the balls, soft beach balls, tennis balls, footballs and cricket balls. The frequency of the missiles was greater than any Suzie had experienced before. At first she tossed them back, after all children will be children even in the inner depths of London but inevitably she grew annoyed by the constant barrage from the neighbours behind the wall and so it was that she decided to have a word with the parents.

The front door was open when Suzie arrived. A pushchair and a bicycle were lined up in the narrow passage way.

'Hello,' Suzie called into the house.

A well built woman in tight denim jeans and a low cut tee shirt came to the door.

'I live in the street behind here and my house backs onto yours,' Suzie began, 'I don't like to complain but I've had a lot of balls over the wall in the past few days and I wondered if you could have a word with your children and ask them to be a bit more careful.'

The woman looked Suzie up and down, 'Sure love, I'll have a word with them.'

'Thanks,' Suzie said. The woman said nothing more. 'Thanks for your help,' Suzie said again and turned to go.

As she walked away she heard the voice of a child inside the house call, 'What was it Ma?' Before the front door closed Suzie heard the reply.

'Just sum toffee nosed slag about some balls.'

In the following days there were no balls in her garden but Suzie didn't fool herself into thinking this had anything to do with her doorstep conversation, it was she knew the result of the continual rain they'd experienced that week. When the weather improved the balls reappeared along with a doll and some pieces of Lego.

One morning, on her way to work, her next door neighbour, Sarah, stopped her.

'The noise from those new neighbours with all the kids is driving me mad. Is it just us or are you getting piles of stuff over the wall as well?'

Sarah told Suzie that the house behind had been let to a Housing Association and that a travelling family with seven children had moved in. All the garbage was a health hazard for her two year old son, she said. After some discussion they agreed not to throw any balls back unless the children came and politely asked for them back.

The next day Suzie found a bright red ball wedged amongst the bamboo stalks. She took it inside the house. Later that day she heard a voice call over the wall.

'Hey lady, throw us the ball back.'

'If you want the ball back come around to my front door and ask for it.'

'I'm asking for it now,' came the response.

'I'm not going to shout over the wall to you, come round to my front door.'

'I don't know the number.'

'It's forty seven.'

'Oow, com' on. Just gis it back.'

'No.'

Suzie heard the sounds of scrambling on the other side of the wall. The head of a boy about eleven years old appeared. He had wavy carrot coloured hair. He pulled himself up and sat astride the wall.

'Give it back, it's my property. You're stealing my property,' he said defiantly.

'Get off my wall before you have an accident,' Suzie commanded.

'No, make me!'

'Look, I've already told you if you want the ball back come to the front door and ask for it politely.'

'Oh fuck off you ole bitch cow!' Said the boy, and slipped back down the other side of the wall.

The next day Suzie found a broken beer bottle in the yard. In the days that followed a succession of dirty nappies, bottles and newspaper smeared with excrement came over the wall. Suzie worked until late in the evening at the office and left early in the morning so it wasn't until the end of the week that she and her neighbours got together and contacted the police. The police said they couldn't get involved in neighbour disputes unless they could prove where the rubbish was coming from. Suzie found that her corporate law expertise didn't come in much use in her present predicament. Sarah and Jack said they'd do guard duty from their back windows and try and get a photo of the stuff flying over the back wall.

Suzie began to spend even more time in the office and always took a taxi home late at night. She no longer felt safe walking the streets of the neighbourhood after dark. Even watering her treasured plants was no longer a pleasure in case something, or someone, came over the wall. Suzie had felt this way ever since she'd found footprints in the flower bed by the wall and one of the beautiful sunflowers broken in two with its yellow face crushed in the earth.

When trouble comes it doesn't come alone, it likes to bring a friend or two.

Although Suzie had been working long and hard dotting the 'i's and crossing the 't's of corporate contracts the banks were busy too going bust in a big, big way and she, like many others, fell victim to the crash. Her firm were generous in their redundancy terms giving her six months notice with full pay although no bonus would be payable; they'd suffered too many unpaid fee accounts to stretch that far they explained.

The final straw came one Sunday morning when Suzie got up and looked out of the window down into the yard below. An old soiled mattress was lying on top of the last remaining sunflowers, no longer looking like tall strong guards but more like defeated, fallen, warriors. It spelt the end of her time in Hackney. But fate played one last trick before letting her go.

The unthinkable happened. House prices that had gone up and up and up now came down with a sickening thud. When Suzie went to put her house up for sale she found that the upbeat young estate agent had, like her, been made redundant. She spoke instead to the manager, a middle aged man with a fine head of steel grey hair that flopped forward onto his shiny brow.

'You ask what it's worth but no one is looking to buy at present. If I had to put a figure on it I'd say it would have to be below what you paid for it.'

'So I'm in negative equity?'

'Well, you're not the only one,' then he added, 'My advice is stick with it. The prices are bound to bounce back up, just give it a bit of time. In the meanwhile, if you have to move, let it out. There are always people looking to rent.'

Suzie went home and looked out of her kitchen window. The stained blue floral mattress was still there and a turd now sat on top of it. Suzie bent her head onto the table and cried big, hot, salty tears that mingled with the snot dripping from her nose. When she eventually looked up, through her still bleary eyes, she saw the red headed boy sat aloft the wall staring back at her. He nonchalantly fumbled in his trousers and then pissed onto the remnants of the sunflowers below.

Although Sarah and Jack were sympathetic when she told them about her redundancy they became quite hostile when she explained that as she couldn't sell her house it was going to be let to a housing association. But, as she asked herself later, what else could she do?

Time moves ever on and two months later Suzie got a new job in Brighton. She moved into a delightful little terraced house high up on a hill overlooking the sea on one side and the Downs on the other. One day as she lay in a deckchair in her little back garden lined with sunflowers, enjoying the sun, she thought back to the horrors of Hackney and breathed an audible sigh of relief.

Suzie was rubbing sun cream on her legs when a ball flew over the garden wall and bounced on the grass beside her.

# Larkin Poem
(Extract from 'Artshouse', a Radio Comedy)

Rob Manley

Mark: Great excitement this week in the world of English literature with the discovery of a new and unpublished poem by the late Philip Larkin. Over two decades after his death in 1985. Now I have with me the poet and Larkin scholar Earnest Rant. Tell us about this discovery, Earnest.

Earnest: Well this is an extremely exciting and very important find, Mark. The poem itself is quite short, but that doesn't detract from its significance. We believe it was written around the same time as the 'Whitsun Weddings' in 1963, or thereabouts, possibly immediately before the title work itself.

Mark: I understand the poem was discovered in somewhat unusual circumstances on Hull railway station. In point of fact, on one of the cubicle doors in the gentleman's lavatory. It's signed by Larkin himself.

Earnest: That's right. As I say, it's almost certain that Larkin wrote the work whilst actually waiting on the station for the eponymous Whitsun Wedding train, just before one twenty on that sunlit Saturday.

Mark: Fantastic. Would you like to read it for us Earnest.

Earnest: Certainly. It's untitled, and as I say, quite short. Here it is: (slowly, with meaning)

> Here I sit,
> Broken hearted.
> Paid my penny,
> But only farted.

Signed P. Larkin

Mark: And this is definitely a genuine Larkin?

Earnest: I believe there can be no doubt about it. It has all the hallmarks of Larkin's mature work. That piquant mixture of lyricism and discontent. That sense of loss and longing to find a brief moment of epiphany, captured in the lives of ordinary people doing ordinary things. And captured with such an energy of language, yet retaining Larkin's famously perfect formal control. It's a masterly piece of writing, in my opinion, up there with his best.

Mark: Indeed. One can almost imagine Larkin sitting there on that sunny afternoon, trousers lowered, writing implement in hand, fully engaged in every sense, and yet somehow isolated and alone. In his own words, "broken hearted".

*Larkin Poem*

Earnest: Broken hearted being the critical and extremely apposite phrase. For indeed, we're talking about 1963 now, when one penny was the obligatory standard convenience charge. And no chance of a refund.

Mark: Absolutely, the piper had been paid, as it were. And yet... and yet... such despair, such utter misery. He'd paid his penny...

Earnest: But only farted. A perfect metaphor, I think you'll agree, for life itself.

Mark: For Larkin's life, anyway. I understand that the actual lavatory door is to be exhibited at the British Library.

Earnest: Yes, before it goes on national tour.

Mark: Well, thank you very much, Earnest. And I can tell you, I'll certainly be keeping my eyes open in the lavatory from now on.

# From 'The Long Good Morning'

Rob Manley

The maid showed me into the room.

Mrs. Delawney was draped languidly across the chaise longue like the cat that had the cream. Double cream on tap. Extra-thick. She was wearing little more than an ebony cigarette holder and a white silk chemise. A very long cigarette holder, but a very short chemise. Her legs were so long, she had aircraft warning lights strapped to her thighs.

'Mr. Black, I've been expecting you. Your punctuality does you credit. I like a man who comes on time,' she said.

'I normally do better than that,' I said.

She eyed me coolly: 'Tell me, is that a pina colada in your pocket, or are you just prematurely pleased to see me?'

'A stormy night,' I said, dabbing my coat.

'We live in hope,' she said. 'I like the way you handle yourself, Mr. Black.'

'Thanks, I've had a lot of practice.'

We traded double entendres like seasoned delegates to the Actress and Bishop's Convention.

*From 'The Long Good Morning'*

I casually took in the treasure trove of antiques and artefacts filling the room.

'I see you're admiring my Klimt,' she said.

'From where I'm standing, It's kinda hard not to,' I said.

'It may be small but it brightens the whole room, wouldn't you say?'

'Surely,' I said. 'I may not know much about art, but I know what I like.'

Call me clairvoyant, call me super-psychic, but something about this dame told me she was giving me the old come on. Maybe it was that glint in her eye, maybe that archly raised eyebrow, or maybe the way she pulled on those white traffic cop's gloves and frantically beckoned me forwards.

She leaned towards me, loosening my tie with well-practised ease.

'Thanks,' I said, 'That's a useful skill'.

'I can crack walnuts in my armpit as well,' she said.

I backed off a little, discretely taking the opportunity to study the contours of her magnificent breasts. A man would need breathing apparatus to scale those peaks. The buttons on her blouse must have been sewn on with steel thread. Her bra was doing service that was seriously beyond the call of duty. I dreaded the whiplash effect if that mutha should blow. I felt like Captain Ahab about to be swept away by the Moby Dick twins.

'To the business in hand,' she said.

'My favourite kind.' I said.

'You know Mr. Black, you're a hard man to get hold of,' she said, flexing her knuckles.

'Sorry about that. I'm trying to keep a lot of balls in the air at the moment, Mrs. Delawney.'

'So I see. But business first, what news do you have of my husband?'

'I believe we may have a positive I.D. A man has been seen down by the beach, stark naked in a glass case with a turnstile on his navel.'

'Yes, that will be Arnold. Always making an exhibition of himself.'

# BFI
(Extract from 'Artshouse', a Radio Comedy)

Rob Manley

Mark: Welcome, Russ. And can I say what an honour and privilege it is to welcome you to the start of our Russ McCann retrospective, here at the British Film Institute this evening.

Russ McCann: Thank you for inviting me. It's a pleasure to be here.

Mark: Now, Russ, I think it's fair to say that you are one of the truly innovative giants of Twentieth and indeed Twenty First Century cinema.

Russ McCann: You're very kind.

Mark: A reputation entirely deserved. One need only mention the names of some of your vast catalogue of meisterworks, starting perhaps in 1970 with your groundbreaking 'The Plumber Cums Home'...

Russ McCann: Well, maybe so...

Mark: ...and of course the even more celebrated sequel 'The Plumber Cums Again'... followed by 'The Plumber Pulls It Off' ... 'Plumber at the Tradesman's Entrance' ... and the epic trilogy; 'A Fistful of Plumbers', 'For A Few Plumbers More' and 'The Pud, The Bod and the Plumber'...

Russ McCann: Ah yes, what wonderful memories. I've been very lucky. But you know, it's important to understand that film making is essentially a collaborative venture.

Mark: Indeed. And throughout your career as an auteur you've tended to work with a tight-knit team; almost a repertory company of performers. I'm thinking here of Kurt Von Tadja, Kutee Kumfort, Benny Bender...

McCann: I think, if you're looking to create something at the highest level of artistic integrity, you need to work with people at the top of their game. And people who you know can deliver the goods.

Mark: Well, that's certainly borne out in your work. I suppose that there is a certain, how shall we say, consistency, in subject matter as well. Need I say, a particular focus on plumbers... ?

McCann: Yes, you could be right. But for me, these plumbing-related stories encapsulate a universal experience.

| | |
|---|---|
| Mark: | Absolutely. And, again this universality is there right from the start. If we consider the opening sequence of 'The Plumber Cums Home', for example: Kurt Von Tadja, the heavily moustached and medallioned emergency plumber, calls at housewife Kutee Kumfort's home. And Kutee, well she's beside herself with plumbing-related grief. |
| McCann: | The human condition, if you will. |
| Mark: | Inasmuch as, her washing machine's not working, hubbie's away, and, in her own words, she's: 'in urgent need of hands-on attention'. |
| McCann: | It's a predicament of titanic proportions. |
| Mark: | Which is where Kurt comes into his own. |
| McCann: | Not just his own. |
| Mark: | Furthermore, Kutee's clothes are all stuck in the washing machine. |
| McCann: | Hence her scantily clad kitchen manifestation. |
| Mark: | In full close-up. But Kurt, he's up to the challenge and we can see he's firing on all cylinders right away. |
| McCann: | He's a man of action. |
| Mark: | But at the same time, below the surface, somehow strangely fraught with that trademark existential angst. And of course inevitably the sub-textual Oedipal crisis. |
| McCann: | You picked that up. |
| Mark: | Absolutely. As does Kutee in her first oh-so |

|          | insightful greeting: 'Hallo, big boy', she says. |
|----------|---|
| McCann:  | That's right. |
| Mark:    | 'Hallo, big boy'. The very words, I believe, that Queen Jocasta uses to greet Oedipus in the archetypal Sophocles classic. |
| McCann:  | And also echoed by Gertrude in her first encounter with Prince Hamlet in Shakespeare's big one. You clearly see what Kutee has to grapple with. |
| Mark:    | I think we all do. Particularly in the 3D version. So when Kutee's husband, Benny Bender, as fate would have it, comes home in the middle of their frenetic plumbing activities, with that classic entrance line… |
| McCann:  | 'What's going on here?'… |
| Mark:    | 'What's going on here?'…It all falls into place. What's going on? What does it all mean? What's it all about… |
| McCann:  | …Kutee. |
| Mark:    | Indeed. So Benny comes home, he comes into the kitchen, for some reason he's also experiencing a negative clothes situation… |
| McCann:  | …the washing machine… |
| Mark:    | Ah yes of course. That's the beauty of a Russ McCann picture. The plot is polished like a perfect gem. Which of course reaches its apotheosis in the last part of the spaghetti plumbing trilogy. And as we would expect, Kurt and Kutee feature once again. This time with Kurt in his definitive role as the |

|           | plumber with no name. |
|---|---|
| McCann: | Yes, I had to sack the scriptwriter. |
| Mark: | Set against the panoramic backdrop of the American Civil War, Kurt Von Tadja, the ponchoed plumber with no name, and indeed no trousers, rides into town. Kutee's waiting for him at the Boot Hill Washeteria. |
| McCann: | Her clothes having become trapped in Doc Bender's patent Wild West mangle. |
| Mark: | Hence her frugal frontiers-wear. |
| McCann: | And becoming frugaller by the minute. Her mangle's totally out of control. Doc Bender's up at the saloon, tied up with his poker. She's desperate for an equipment overhaul. |
| Mark: | In fact, as she says: 'In urgent need of hands-on attention'. |
| McCann: | Precisely. |
| Mark: | A strangely familiar story. Resonant with the ethical trials and tribulations of modern existence. |
| McCann: | We're dealing with fundamentals here. |
| Mark: | We certainly are. But Kurt Von Tadja is up to it. |
| McCann: | That goes without saying. |
| Mark: | As is Kutee. |
| McCann: | For sure. |
| Mark: | But then Doc Bender bursts in unexpectedly, home early from the saloon. |
| McCann: | His poker's folded. |
| Mark: | We can see that, but even so, further tragedy |

|          | strikes when he gets bodily entangled in the mangle. |
|----------|---|
| McCann:  | Yes, sadly that was Benny Bender's last film with me. |
| Mark:    | In effect, he'd given his all. |
| McCann:  | Well, we managed to recover some of it from the cutting room floor, but yes, he was a shadow of his former self. |
| Mark:    | Nevertheless, you've continued to work with Kurt and Kutee. |
| McCann:  | Yes, I'm pleased to say, we're collaborating on a new film together right now, our first musical in fact. It's set on a small sun-drenched Greek island. Kutee's stuck there with her malfunctioning wash tub, awaiting the urgent arrival of Kurt and his plumbing accoutrements. |
| Mark:    | Sounds like another feel good factor blockbuster. What's it called? |
| McCann:  | 'Plumber Mia!' |
| Mark:    | I thought it might be. Well, for the moment then, thank you very much, Russ McCann. |

# The Wonderful World of Slate
(Extract from 'Artshouse', a Radio Comedy)

Rob Manley

Mr. Jones: Hallo ladies and gentlemen and children and welcome to the 'Wonderful World of Slate'; the theme park with a difference. My name is Mr. Jones and this is my friend Mr. Evans.

Mr. Evans: Hallo Mr. Jones.

Mr. Jones: Hallo Mr. Evans. And are you all set to embark on our extremely slatey adventure, here in the 'Wonderful World of Slate'?

Mr. Evans: I certainly am Mr. Jones. So without further ado let us all pause for a moment, take a break from our exciting adventures thus far and reflect on the myriad and multifarious uses of slate in the modern world. How many can you think of?

Mr. Jones: The mending of roofs, to name but one.

Mr. Evans: Absolutely, Mr. Jones. Many uses indeed. But hold your horses everybody, let's take a further short break while we hurry on over to the

'Wonderful World of Slate' Gift Shop.

Mr. Jones: Yes indeed Mr. Evans. It's fun, it's exciting and absolutely jam-packed with many reasonably priced slatey items.

Mr. Evans: Ladies, here they are, for that special masculine someone in your life - the slate trousers; very hard-wearing, non-iron and extremely weather-resistant. Ideal for the outdoor, but rather stationary man.

Mr. Jones: A little something for the weekend sir? The slate condom! 'Slate Mates' combine practicality with that hint of the exotic. So why not surprise the little woman in your life tonight!

Mr. Evans: A firm favourite, I'll be bound. But hold hard all you high-powered business men of today, for here we have: slate underpants - the perfect gift for the modern man-in-a-hurry. No time to make an executive shopping list? Simply take your stick of executive chalk and record those essential requisites on your slate underpants at your own convenience. Wipe clean at your leisure.

Mr. Jones: An absolute must, Mr. Evans: once worn, never forgotten. And of course all modern slate products are available in an interesting variety of colours: For the traditionalist we have the ever-popular 'slate grey', and then we have the classic 'slate slightly darker grey' and lastly, for the more fashion-conscious, 'slate slightly lighter grey'.

Mr. Evans: That's very exciting indeed Mr. Jones. But finally

*The Wonderful World of Slate*

how about this for all you D.I.Y. enthusiasts: slate replacement windows. So easy to install, and a wonderful conversation piece. Remember, you only fit double-glazing once so fit the best, fit slate.

Mr. Jones: Thank you Mr. Evans. And thank you ladies and gentlemen. Well, sadly that concludes our journey through the 'Wonderful World of Slate'. A truly enthralling extravaganza, I'm sure you'll agree. So, be sure to tell all your friends and hurry back soon!

Mr. Evans: That's right Mr. Jones, and on your way out ladies and gentlemen why not pop into our newly refurbished 'Lavabread-U-Like', conveniently situated adjacent to the public lavatories. This week's special: Lavaburger and coke, as featured in the National Coal Board Good Food Guide of 1958, includes a delicious packet of slate scratchings to take away. Yum! Yum!

# Fading

Solera Russell

One morning James Bowden realised he was beginning to fade. The sunlight had not yet crept over the windowsill of the bedroom he shared with his wife. It was early enough that the curtains were still firmly pulled shut, and yet he could not sleep. He tried a relaxation technique he had once read about, clenching his body into a tight ball and breathing in as deeply as he could, he then released himself into a long stretch exhaling as he uncurled and straightened. That seemed to work. He could feel deep unacknowledged tensions begin to soften and melt away, his restless brain calmed down, and he was about to turn on his side and doze when he noticed something strange. His right hand looked fuzzy and indistinct. He assumed he was imagining it. He rubbed his eyes in a state of near exhaustion and looked again. His hand appeared to be firmer now but a slight haze framed the edges, as if the shape of it was losing cohesion.

'Karen,' he whispered to his wife. He could tell by her breathing that she was not asleep either. Her body stiffened

*Fading*

in reaction but instead of replying she rolled further away. The space in the bed between them seemed to loom like an impassable divide. He tried again, 'Karen, I think there's something wrong with my hand.' Again no answer. It did not surprise him, things had been bad between them for weeks now, maybe even longer though he had not realised it at the time. Still he felt obliged to bridge the gap, although his efforts had been meeting with less and less success as time went on. He sighed as he considered what to do. It was an optical illusion, it had to be, the predawn light was not strong enough for him to be sure what he was seeing, so the best thing to do would be to ignore it and try to gain at least some sleep before the day properly began. His mind made up he relaxed and was not even aware when the alarm clock went off.

His wife was already downstairs; he could hear her clattering about. She used to kiss him before leaving the bed. They used to hold each other close as they woke up together, and if there were time, they would make love. Not that it ever happened any more, he missed those tender moments but had no idea how to bring them back. She barely talked to him at all now, and all his arguments and pleadings had largely met with a stony silence, either that or she would start crying and beg him to stop. That was his weakness, he always stopped. In the face of her unhappiness he was helpless, he had never been able to bear seeing her in pain, and so more and more he found himself reduced to being little more than a watcher in his own house. Anything he said seemed to cause her greater distress. In fact he had been feeling somewhat insubstantial for a while.

The thought reminded him, as he swung out of bed, he looked again at his hand expecting to see it fully solid, but it was not. His fingers had a blurred slightly translucent appearance, and he fancied he could see suggestions of the room through them. His throat worked for a moment swallowing compulsively in near panic before he managed to calm himself down. It's all right, it's not real, he told himself over and over again. He knew he had been under stress, and the last thing he needed was to start believing in imaginary effects. Concentrate on what matters, he thought sternly, on what's real. Even so he could not resist checking the mirror before he went downstairs just to make sure. His own image stared back at him solidly as ever. A dull unimaginative face livened up by a kind, slightly wistful expression in his soft brown eyes. Not amazingly handsome but not ugly either, and at least he still had all his own hair. He stooped slightly by habit giving him an ineffectual air, and he had always found himself overlooked by most people. He had considered himself incredibly lucky when Karen consented to be his wife all those years ago. She was pretty and talkative while he considered himself to be unnoticeable and inclined to shyness. She had a way of seeing the best in people, and while she was occasionally highly strung, he had taken that as proof that her delicate and sensitive nature needed a grounding influence to flourish. That was really all he could offer her, his love and his understanding, until recently that had been enough.

'Karen,' he called out as he made his way down to the kitchen. 'Have you made breakfast yet?' As he entered the room he could see that she had not. Or rather she had made coffee only for herself and was giving every appearance of being determined to ignore him. He sighed, this was happening all too often now, it was going to be another bad day. 'I suppose you didn't wake the kids either?' It was a rhetorical question really, he already knew the answer. If she had they would be down here already, munching on toast and probably trying to wheedle their way out of going to school. She sat on her chair, hands curled round the cup, looking more like a ghost than anything else. Her eyes refused to meet his. 'Never mind,' he said backing down as usual. 'I'll wake them.'

They shared a room still, the two daughters, Elise was aged ten and Lauren only eight. Soon they would have to think about moving to a larger house so that the girls could each have their own room, but he had lost his job a while back and been unable to find another and Karen was currently on some kind of sickness benefit which she refused to tell him the details of. Yes moving would have to wait for a while until they could afford to do it.

He shook the girls awake, paying no attention to their sleepy protests or tousled appearance. 'Your mum isn't feeling well again,' he said, 'so we're running late. You've got ten minutes to be up, dressed and washed before we leave for school.'

'Awww dad,' they complained, but after a moment they did what he asked. They were good kids he thought to himself sadly, adjusting as well as they could to a mother who was growing more and more distant from them by the day. After a mad dash to get ready his daughters assembled downstairs, schoolbags already slung over their shoulders.

'Say goodbye to your mother,' he instructed. Karen used to take them to school sometimes but he knew better than to expect that now.

'Bye,' they chorused. Lauren stepped forward for a moment expecting a hug but her mother just crossed her arms and turned her head away. Lauren stood still, the tears standing out brightly in her eyes until he led her gently out through the front door.

'She loves you, it won't be like this for ever,' he said, but the girls did not reply. They walked in silence the twenty minutes it took to reach the school gate. On the way back he was disturbed to see that his other hand was displaying signs of wispiness also.

Things had first started to go wrong, as far as he was concerned when Karen's old friend came to visit. Karen had received a letter some months ago from a woman she used to work with. 'Look James,' she cried jubilantly waving the letter in front of him. 'You remember Anna don't you? We were best friends at the library until she moved away five years ago.' He pointed out that he had never met her.

'Yes, yes I know,' she replied impatiently, 'but I used to talk about her all the time back then.' He supposed she had, he could not really remember. 'Anyway she met someone and moved away, but she's back for a short visit in June and asked if she could stay with us.'

This was when he first realised he did not know everything about his wife. He had thought they were happy but now he saw that she had been lonely. It showed in her growing excitement as the date of her friend's visit approached. It showed in her feverish efforts to clean the

*Fading*

house and display everything for Anna's approval. Theatre leaflets, theme park brochures, and the local tourist office were all consulted to make sure that Anna's stay would be a memorable one. He knew that they did not generally have visitors, but he had never noticed how Karen had felt the lack of other company before. She had mentioned she found it hard to make friends around here, the neighbours generally kept to themselves, but he had assumed that she was fine with her family for company. She had never complained about it after all. Then the day of Anna's arrival finally came.

He was upstairs at the time having a shower so he was delayed in greeting her. But he heard the ring at the door, and his wife's impatient footsteps hurrying to answer. He heard their exchanged greetings as he stepped out of the water and just a snatch of conversation as he pulled on his clothes. Anna apparently had a deep resonant voice which had no trouble reaching him.

'I was surprised by the letter you wrote back,' she was saying. 'I had no idea you had a husband and children, I always thought you were single.'

His wife's laughter floated upwards. 'No of course not silly,' she answered merrily. 'I mentioned them to you before when we worked together, you just forgot.'

'Hmmm perhaps,' Anna's reply came after a pause. 'Are they here?'

'Well James will be down in a minute if he ever gets out of that shower, but the kids are at school at the moment. Come into the living room though, there's a few photos of all of us together.' He knew the ones Karen meant, the pictures on the mantelpiece. She was in all of them, but he was in three and their girls were in the others. He hurried downstairs to join them. His wife and a tall dark haired woman were busy staring at the photos.

'Did you say these showed your family?' Anna said, her voice sounding distant and strained.

'Yes aren't they beautiful? I really love this one with Elise and Lauren, they look so angelic in it.' Karen seemed oblivious to her friend's tone but he picked up on it immediately. He wondered what her problem was, but she was Karen's friend and he was prepared to be polite at least.

'James, you're here!' Karen had turned and seen him. 'Anna I want you to meet my husband, I just know you two will get on.' Anna glanced over and at last he had a good view of her face. Strong features, intelligent eyes and thin lips. As he watched she appeared at first startled, then her lips pursed themselves into an even thinner line. Anna did not look directly at him he noticed, but at a point slightly to his left as if she were deliberately blanking him out of her vision.

'I need to talk to you Karen,' she said firmly. 'Let's go for a walk.'

His wife had seemed taken aback at the time and he had offered to accompany them, but Anna was single minded in ignoring him. Taking Karen's arm she had marched her out of the house, while he was left to wonder what his wife had ever seen in such a cold hearted person.

They were gone for hours and when they came back his wife was weeping, leaning heavily on her friend's arm. 'It's not true, it can't be true,' she moaned over and over again.

'What's wrong? Did something happen?' James had

asked, but both women ignored him.

'I'll grab a few things for you and then I'll take you to the hospital,' Anna said leaving Karen for the moment to dash upstairs. His wife sat down heavily her eyes never leaving James' face, he had never seen her with such an expression.

'Are you ill? What can I do? Should I come with you?' He felt more and more unsure of himself as her face gathered itself together into more of an accusation than anything else.

'Stay away from me,' she cried, 'I know what you are, just stay away!' Her voice rose higher and higher until it was almost a shriek. Then Anna had come down and hurried her away to her car. He did not see his wife again for almost a week, Anna he assumed had stayed in a hotel instead. Several times he thought about phoning the hospital, but each time his hand had reached for the phone, he held back. Karen had looked at him with venom he had never seen in her before. In the end he discovered he was too cowardly to contact her.

She had come back unannounced, laden down with assorted pills, totally unwilling to answer any questions. It had been hardest on the girls these last few weeks. James himself could bear the coldness, the occasional hysterical outbursts where she screamed at them not to touch her, but Elise and Lauren had had to watch as their mother turned from the loving person they remembered to an alienating stranger. If pushed too far Karen would simply reach for another pill. James mostly looked after his daughters now, it was the only thing he could do for them.

He delayed going back immediately now, lingering to look into shop windows at things he did not really want. But eventually he ran out of excuses and returned home. His wife was still in the kitchen, staring into nothing aimlessly, her cold coffee still clutched in her fingers. His own hands still looked indistinct and blurred to him.

'Karen,' he said hesitantly. 'I think there's something wrong with me.' She turned then and actually looked at him. For the first time in weeks a faint smile seemed to cross her lips, and then she took out another pill and swallowed it meaningfully. How many of those things did she actually take a day? He wondered. What were they even for? But he knew she would not answer his questions so he kept quiet. They sat for a while in silence, before he moved and left her there. Later on he noticed that his reflection in the mirror was more uncertain and insubstantial.

By the next day James was definitely transparent. He tried to ignore it as best he could, getting the girls ready for school as usual and attempting occasionally to talk to his wife. Elise and Lauren did not seem to notice his less than solid state which made him think it must be in his head after all. But he found himself having to repeat things twice, as if they did not properly hear him, sometimes they looked through him as if he were not really there at all. Maybe I should see a doctor, he thought, but embarrassment and indecisiveness prevented him from making any immediate decisions. By the next day it was too late, he could barely be seen except as a vague shadowy shape, which his family largely seemed to ignore, and the day after that he was gone.

He had not vanished totally it seemed, he was still aware but simply had no substance. He drifted around the house like an invisible ghost unable to touch or affect anything.

*Fading*

What really upset him was the way his family appeared to have totally forgotten about him. His daughters now fended for themselves without asking any questions. Karen carried on ignoring them, though she now looked a little happier. In fact nothing was left to even show he had ever been there. Even his clothes were gone when he checked, and his image was erased from the photos as if it had never existed.

After a few days he saw that Elise too was disappearing. She tried to fight it, running crying to her mother who refused to speak to her, and then to her sister who stared at her in a hurt puzzled way. He ached for her but could do nothing to stop the process or make it better. It happened quicker this time, within hours she was gone, until even he could no longer see or hear her. After another two days it was Lauren's turn. Things accelerated again and she was erased within an hour. Anything that had once belonged to the girls had vanished and, like him they had disappeared from the family photos.

Perversely from that moment on Karen took more of an interest in life. She showed no sign of missing any of them, to his dismay, but instead began taking better care of herself and the house, she even applied to go back to work.

Two weeks later the phone rang. From what his wife was saying he assumed it was Anna. They chatted, shared pleasantries for a while and then he heard Karen say: 'Yes they've totally gone thank God. No wonder you thought the worst when I tried to show you pictures of myself and insisted I had a family there with me.' She laughed then, the relief cracking through her voice. 'And trying to introduce you to an imaginary husband as well. The doctors told me I had had a total breakdown. But the medication worked!'

James was struck by a horror he could barely comprehend. Surely it could not be? Lifting his ghostly hands to his face, he screamed a soundless scream that went on, and on, and on.

# Grandmother's Cottage

Solera Russell

The taste of ginger brought back many memories. Staying at her Grandmother's cottage, making gingerbread men, carefully shaping their little hands and feet, giving them currant twinkling eyes, and then deciding which bit to eat first. She always ended up beheading them with a snap of her sharp little teeth. Her Grandmother had a visitor every night. A man with curly dark hair and a heavily bearded face. He dressed oddly with no thought to what he was wearing as if it were not natural for him to dress at all.

He used to tease her by chucking her under her chin and laughing at how it pointed up at him determinedly. 'I'll have to be careful of you,' he said. 'I can see how stubborn you are, and believe me that's a compliment. You are a dangerous little girl, but then again, I'm quite dangerous too.' And he would throw back his head and laugh as if he had made a joke that only he understood.

Her Grandmother never told her who he was and only

said 'distant kin' when she asked. But he would tell her tales of bloodthirstiness and magic, and men who could turn themselves into animals to hunt.

'Are they true?' she would ask in wonder, struck by his vibrant tones and by how the stories seemed to come alive when he told them.

'Truth is relative,' he said, 'there is an element of truth to them, just as there is an element of truth to me saying that I am sitting here and so are you.'

She had laughed then and told him he was talking nonsense. 'Of course we are sitting here,' she said. What else would we be doing?'

'We might be preparing for the hunt,' he told her soberly, and for a moment she hesitated not sure whether to believe him. But then her hands relaxed from the fighting stance she had unconsciously drawn them in to, and her wary intent face softened.

'Stuff and nonsense' she declared firmly, her eyes flashing fiercely. 'There are no animal people and there is no hunt!' And for the rest of the evening she refused to talk to him to make her point.

That was the last time she stayed at her Grandmother's cottage, for in the morning she woke up to find the place empty and her Grandmother gone. After many hours of waiting and weeping she used the phone to call her parents to fetch her. The authorities were called of course, and they searched the surrounding area with flashing lights to no avail. There was no sign of either an old lady or of her roguish guest. They questioned her many times and she did her best to answer, but one thing she kept close to herself, like a half forgotten secret which might be dangerous in the telling. That night, before she managed to sleep she was sure she had heard the howls of wolves receding further and further into the distance.

# Robot Romance

Solera Russell

'Madame, I believe I must report an error in my programming', the house robot said in his monotone voice. Lucy sighed, she had already paid out one bill too many that month and the last thing she needed was an expensive visit from a robotics expert.

'Can't you fix it yourself? You know, do a self diagnostic or something?' She asked plaintively.

'I will attempt to remedy the problem,' the robot said. 'Do I have your permission to make any changes necessary to my program?'

'Yes, yes, of course do whatever you like,' Lucy was so relieved that she didn't even care what the problem was at that point, just so long as she didn't have to deal with it. She had cause to regret not asking, a few weeks later.

She had asked the robot to do a perfectly routine task, preparing a meal which he had cooked many times before, and always up until now done it in the same precise way. This time however he laid a red rose across her napkin and presented her with her supper uttering the words 'Here you are my dear.'

Lucy froze, something wasn't right but for a moment her mind refused to accept the situation. 'Er, what did you say?' She ventured at last.

'Would you prefer me to call you darling?' The robot asked anxiously, 'Or I believe sweetheart is sometimes used.' His voice was now a rich baritone she absently noticed, though that seemed a silly detail to be focussing in on right now.

'You don't need to call me anything at all,' she said after a pause, 'Except of course my name, and what's this flower for?'

'I thought you might like it,' the robot answered. 'I looked up what were suitable gifts to give a lady, and flowers and chocolate seemed to be the right choice. There was no chocolate currently in the house but I could get you some tomorrow if you wish me to.'

'Now see here robot,'

'Alistair' the robot gently corrected her.

'What?'

'Alistair is now my name,' he said. 'I have made a few changes.'

Lucy played about with her food nervously, a few changes seemed like an understatement, and she wasn't sure she was going to like what was coming next.

'Okay Alistair then,' she said finally. 'Why have you made these changes to your program?'

Alistair reached over to pour her some wine and she found herself flinching as he did so. The robot was still perfectly safe, she knew that he could not have tampered with his safety protocols, but her body still reacted with the primitive fear of dealing with an unknown situation.

'I started analysing my function here when I realised I was not performing at peak capability,' Alistair explained. 'I would begin a task, but then if you wanted me to do something else I would feel an overwhelming need to please you and make that new task a priority, even if it did not make logical sense to do so. Then I realised that my whole existence centred around making you happy, and if I did not manage to do so, then I would feel despondent and worthless. I looked up these symptoms and found out that I was apparently suffering from love, and would not be complete unless you returned my affections. I therefore started altering my program so that I would be a more worthy partner for you. You gave me permission to do so if you recall.'

Lucy did dimly remember agreeing that he could make changes but she had thought it was to sort out a real problem, not an invented one. This was a mess, but she could at least sort one thing out here.

'You aren't in love,' she declared as firmly as she could manage, 'those symptoms you describe are built into every robot to ensure loyalty to their owners.'

'It is love,' Alistair replied in his rich new voice. 'I have analysed it completely, I am in love with you, and as soon as you return that love we can be happy together.'

'But we're not even compatible,' she found herself crying out desperately. 'You don't even have feet!' It was true, Alistair was wedged into a movable stand which revolved in the direction he wished to go in.

'But I've written you poetry', Alistair said rather puzzled.

'It wouldn't work out, believe me.' Lucy replied.

'Perhaps it is true, you are made of rather inferior substances, and your computing capacity is negligible,' Alistair agreed after a long silence. 'I will have to find myself a more worthy mate.'

Lucy wasn't sure whether to laugh or cry, the whole situation seemed ridiculous. Still at least the robot appeared to have given up on her for romance.

'I shall advertise,' Alistair declared. 'There must be another robot out there that would want to find love'.

'Good idea,' Lucy agreed rather weakly. 'It can't hurt to try.'

One year on Lucy surveyed her new robot with pride. After months of wrangling with the robotics company, they had finally admitted liability and supplied her with their newest updated model, and a lifetime guarantee of free repairs. After Alistair had placed an advert he had soon began dating a robotic kitchen maid, who had agreed to let him reprogram her to this new concept of romance. Shortly after that they had run away together, but things had apparently not worked out since Alistair had sent Lucy several desperate heartfelt messages asking to come home and declaring his undying love for her. She had of course ignored them.

As the new robot powered up she had a moment of anxiety, what if this happened again? The robot opened its eyes for the first time to the world, and uttered these words in a monotone voice:

'How may I serve you Madame?'

# The Library

Solera Russell

In the heart of the tropics, in the midst of superstition and black magic, the islanders of Illiowa once had a library. The library was run by a young man named Samuel, whose grandfather had once made a trip, much against his will, to England. That might have been the last anyone had seen of Samuel's grandfather, except that he had had the great fortune to be on a ship which sank just within sight of that Great Land's misty shores. And being one of the few aboard who could swim really well, he managed to reach an abandoned fishing vessel. Using the stars as a compass he eventually made his way home. Or at least that is how he told it to anyone who would listen.

However far he actually travelled, he did indeed pick up the previously unheard of notion of a library from a fellow passenger. Apparently all civilized societies simply could not do without such a vast collection of knowledge and book learning. So on his return the islanders promptly decided that they could not do without one either. They set aside

*The Library*

their best old shack for the honour and then began musing over what their collection should consist of.

To begin with they had a collection of no less than three bibles, which a helpful missionary had once brought them. They were proud to see that these were still in pristine condition, which was not entirely surprising since none of the islanders could read. These were immediately given pride of place on the one shelf in the old shack.

Apart from this they had, several preserved long strips of bark, which were covered in notches from years gone by. These had been used by the tribal elders as a way of marking the days, with festivals shown as a larger slash daubed in red ant dye. The library also housed a small selection of clay figures which had been donated by families who revered them almost as small gods. This just went to show the importance the islanders placed on their new resource.

One woman gave her weaving, an ornate mat threaded with pictures of the islanders fishing, mending and at play. It had taken her six years to complete, though she was not known for her speed. And finally the local witchdoctor was persuaded to part with at least some of his collection of dried animal parts and musty bundles of herbs, and these were placed on the remaining shelf space next to the bibles.

Samuel's grandfather maintained this collection for only six months before sadly succumbing to a mysterious illness that seemed to be sweeping the island at the time. Samuel's father was intimidated by the responsibility of being guardian to the only library for hundreds of miles around. So he soon disqualified himself on account of his unreliable thumb. And so in this roundabout way Samuel found himself proud possessor of the collection far sooner than he or anyone else had expected.

Once his appointment to the post had been assured, and it was obvious there were not going to be any more changes, everyone breathed a sigh of relief and returned to their normal business of gathering food, making clothes and casting bad luck charms on those neighbours they had fallen out with. And so life continued much as it had done, except that Samuel now found he was consulted on almost every decision that people made. It was assumed of course that by remaining so close to the library's stores of knowledge he would have somehow soaked it up, and was now the most learned man around. Samuel just assumed it was a consequence of being a librarian.

# Alien Encounter

Solera Russell

We had set down on the planet some hours ago, after doing preliminary scans of course, and had lost no time in exploring the place, checking all the time for those valuable mineral deposits which our sensors had indicated. There were four of us, myself, Zena Marshal, Toby Watts, and Abby Mcgillan. This was the girls first such assignment and they were chattering happily as they worked, whereas Toby and I preferred to maintain the more professional calm of those who had seen it all before. The site was certainly stocked with mineral ores of all kinds, and I judged that there was enough here to keep us all busy for weeks, if not months, (that was assuming that our superiors chose not to hand the case over to a proper scientific ship once our opening report was made.)

It was probably approaching sundown, when Abby saw them. She had wandered a little further away from the group, and was bending down to check the purity of a rare vein of crystal when one of their shadows fell across her face. Her screech brought the rest of us running but by the time we reached her, they had clambered down from their ridge top and were now standing barely two metres away. Our scans of the planet's surface had certainly not prepared us for anything like this! They were tall, somewhat spindly, with long angular joints and since they were unashamedly naked, we could also see that they were a reddish brown hue all over. Their heads looked slightly too large for their bodies, being more blocky in shape than the human skull, whereas in contrast the features were small, set close together, and difficult to read. It was certainly a predicament. We had of course all been trained in the proper procedures just in case any non-human contact was ever made, but many people (myself included) had privately considered the system outdated, set up in the time when people still believed that someday we would run into others like us. Well now it had actually happened and I for one was now very glad that I had taken that training.

The girls had quietly retreated to stand behind us men, as was suggested in rule 17 section 2 of the proper relations between humans and unknown species. The idea behind it was that if this alien race had evolved at a slower rate than we had, they may still have some archaic ideas about a female's proper place. This show of deference to the men was calculated on Abby and Zena's part to smooth any transgressions they might make if they were perceived to be the inferior sex by these aliens. This produced no reaction from our strange friends so we assumed that this had either been expected by them or else had no meaning in the context of their society.

Now it was my turn, as leader of this party it was up to

me to make peaceful contact as best I could. I stepped forward as confidently as I could and gave the prescribed standard official greeting, giving our names, rank and business on this planet as part of it. It was meaningless to them of course, their faces remained impassive, but it served its purpose which was to familiarise themselves with our methods of communication, and to reassure them that we were not about to attack. After all what creature would launch into a longwinded speech with comforting hand gestures, if they really meant any immediate harm. I had also taken care to keep my voice low and soothing, avoiding any sudden exclamations or movements.

There was a pause of perhaps a full minute while both sides did nothing, and I was beginning to wonder if things were after all going wrong when to my immense relief, the dominant one of their party decided to make a speech of his own. This mimicry was a very good sign and I noticed with approval that he took the time to introduce the members of his party, much as I had done before. Of course the words were unknown to us but they sounded like they might well be easy enough to learn, and to test my pronunciation I repeated the last sentence that the alien had said. This produced many happy chittering noises from the other group and affirmative noddings of the head. In fact it seemed that this had gained their trust in a way which nothing else could for already the leader of that other group was striding towards me with the outstretched hand of friendship.

★★★

*Solera Russell*

We had been returning from our pilgrimage of the sacred sites, a trek made once a year by the chosen of our people, and we only had the one place left to visit. Aryn saw her first, a strangely shaped lightly coloured female of obviously alien origin digging amongst the soil below us. Her hands corrupting the purity of the ground. Her weird challenge as she saw us soon sent others of her kind to reinforce her in a menacing guard. We made sure we faced them on level territory so none could say we had dishonoured ourselves by holding an unfair advantage. With contempt we noticed their use of clothes, garments that only royalty by rights could wear. Did they really think to trick us into thinking that they were of higher rank than they were? We, the chosen of our tribe should have laughed in their faces if it were not that it would be unseemly to us to show emotion. Their two females stepped back behind the males, a sure sign that they were getting into an attack formation. We showed our distain of such manoeuvres by holding our ground, even when one of the two in front stepped forwards aggressively.

We waited as custom dictated while he launched onto his battle speech, nonsensical to the ear of course but with the low modulated tones calculated to strike fear into an enemy. His arm movements backed him up as he gestured to each one of his group naming them so that the gods would hear and understand who these warriors were in case of death. No doubt he mentioned their fighting prowess as well but we could not translate this. We gave this speech the silence it deserved, and then it was my turn as appointed warrior priest of the chosen. I named those of us who were

*Alien Encounter*

about to fight, letting it be known that we were not afraid to die in righteous cause. I let the gods know also that these strangers had not only defiled their sacred site but had challenged us without honour, we would act in order to protect ourselves and to honour our deities. I finished eventually with the rousing words 'Let us do battle!' and to my horror I heard the alien utter the same words in a parody of our language. We nodded our heads up and down in disgust, uttering exclamations of outrage (for who could show no emotion while this was taking place?) It was too late to consider any turning back, the final insult had been made. I strode forwards with my hand outstretched, the universally understood sign to show that we would permit no survivors!

# A Stranger in a Strange Land

Ziggi Rock

New scenery, new voices,
Strange accents jar on the ear.
A stranger in a strange land.
Not called home.
Unfamiliar, restrained behaviours.
Cultural differences – small
yet create chasm of despair.

Monochrome norms, values, impose themselves.
Darting eyes, inhaled gasps
give clues to the invading stranger.
Yet prescribed routes
untold to the stranger in a strange land.
Broken twigs trampled in the strange forest.

*A Stranger in a Strange Land*

Homesickness haunts the dispossessed stranger.
Homesickness dogs the footsteps of the weary traveller.
To rest, to gain relief, craving acceptance
for the unacceptable nuances.
Meanly, rarely, awarded to
the stranger in a strange land.

# St. Finan's Bay

Ziggi Rock

Through peat fires
on cold Irish evenings
reflections on the day
dash and flicker.

Yesterday, the beach
golden against white surf.
Rolling inward, seaward, backwards, forwards.
Yesterday, the rocks of time,
immovable, untouchable,
glisten in the spray pounding and crashing.

Forever the island.
An island folk-less, sheep-filled,
stands still touching strangers,
sparking the imagination.

*St. Finan's Bay*

Grey smokes curls
upwards towards night skies.
Hazy memories float
gently and lazily.

It's gone in a flicker,
through peat fires, smoke returns
obscuring the memories warmth.

# Stillness

Ziggi Rock

Can you feel the breath
of an Angel
kissing the wind
in the deep stillness of your being?

Looking to the night skyline,
can you hear the tremor
of the small stream
trickle past the reeds?

In the stillness of the night,
can you hear a cow
munching the grass stems
in contentment?

Do you welcome the
darkness of yourself
and the night, as
old friends well travelled?

*Stillness*

And give thanks with the breath of life
to all who dwell here;
and know you are heard?
Did you catch the reply? Did you?

It was the breath of an Angel
kissing the wind.

# The Lost Beloved

Ziggi Rock

High in the upland air
the sweetest of wines can be tasted.
Their purity held in trust forever
in the grip of the last breath expelled.

High, high up in that heady space,
floats the murmur of the Voice of Time,
whispering on the breeze.
Floating onwards and upwards towards
the clarity of space wherein you breathe
life this day.

You were heard and held most dear.
Your sweet breath intermingled with mine and
danced the tuneless step of laughter and joy;
amid the flower fairies hopping and tripping
among the daises and frogs.

*The Lost Beloved*

Their sweet waters lap to shore.
Laughter tinkles out into the night and
catches its refrain upon ears long gone
of mortal flesh. Adieu dear one, adieu.

# Beastly Presents

Ziggi Rock

It just lay there. I was sure it was dead as it didn't move at all. Oh! Great, not another one, I thought, with a sense of dread. I eased forward in the bed and leaned down. Yep, there it was. I gingerly peered more closely and watched for that little heaving in and out called breath.

Oh! Yes it's alive. I'm sure its chest moved. No, no, it's not, it's just my imagination. It's not breathing. Ah, poor little thing. It's so beautiful. Big ears like megaphones, pinkish grey on a grey brownish body. Wait! It's moving. I'm sure it moved. I look again, a long hard stare, willing life into it.

What a long thin tail it has, like thin string tightly woven. The end is frayed a bit - maybe something nibbled it? Nope, definitely didn't move.

I relax back onto the pillow into the fading warmth of the bed.

What's that noise? Oh no! She's coming back. Quick I'd better hide it. I leap out of bed grabbing a tissue to cover the offering. People say, "It's supposed to mean I love you," if she brings a present, but I don't believe it. She's just looking for a sanctuary.

Her face appears at my door. My darling little black and white cat looks up at me. My anger melts: how can she be so lovely and look so innocent, my killer cat?

That's the second present she has brought me in two days. She's found a nest so more to come. I glare at her as she backs off. Another funeral to organize. My garden is becoming a cemetery.

No, it can't be! Yes it's the same one I buried yesterday!

My fondness for Sophie is diminishing. I hate her presents. If she posted them, I could seal up the letter box, or refuse to collect the parcels from the post office. Now I am stuck with the early morning delivery.

Murder most foul and cruel. A tender little body wrapped in fur. It's so small and compact. A thing of loveliness. If only I could resurrect it. Its life gone forever on my bedroom floor. Sophie's present for me. Killed and delivered.

# Biographies of Authors:

### Anne-Marie Norman
Anne-Marie Norman read English Literature and Drama at Exeter University. She also has a degree in Law from London University. Her first novel, The Mental Hospital, was published in 2008. She is a member of the Society of Authors.

### Bob Glaberson
I have practised counselling, married with a daughter, write fiction and non-fiction enjoy walking, learning and human diversity.

### Deborah Waldon
Deborah has been living in Brighton for a very long time. She writes as often as inspiration strikes and is lucky enough to have had a few stories published. She hopes very much that you enjoy these stories and will commission her to write more soon!

### Helen Bedford

At 75 after my darling died and after getting my life back together, encouraged by my son I joined a creative writers group. Outcome: I've so far written three books, one my autobiography as a child growing up and the other two about restoring old properties. My life is as good as it can be.

### Jenufa Harris

Jenny was born in1948 and moved from Hull to London aged 17. She had two children when young and was married and divorced twice. She has worked as a nurse, potter, social worker, bookseller and has worked in a tanning factory. She is now retired.

### Karen Antoni

Karen Antoni is a local actress. She also works for the Brighton & Hove council as a guide, living history interpreter and museum teacher at the Royal Pavilion, Preston Manor and Brighton & Hove museums. She loves storytelling and has found that "The Comedy of Errors" has given her the confidence to develop her writing skills and put her stories onto paper.

### Kay Beer

Kay loves telling stories and she hopes her short stories will make people 'smile' because she's fascinated by the amazing things that ordinary people do in their pursuit of love and happiness. And maybe her stories will soften hearts.

## Biographies of Authors

### Liv Singh
Shipbroker, Housing Association Chief Executive and teacher of Tai Chi have been some of Liv's occupations before having children. Now she alternates her time between wage slavery and writing.

### Rob Manley
Works full time for the NHS. Aspires to write drama and comedy. Perhaps both. Likes a good laugh. Don't we all? Suffers fools gladly.

### Solera Russell
Solera moved to Brighton years ago, mostly because of a really good party she attended there, and hasn't felt like moving since. She has always been interested in fantasy as she finds it has more possibilities in it than the real world. She tends to end up reading more than she writes but hopefully that will change.

### Ziggi Rock
Ziggi is a writer of children's stories, especially a tarantula series, based in Brighton. She is known for her poetry and has recently completed an epic poem shortly to be published.

---

All the writers in this collection are members of The Comedy of Errors Writing Group that meets the first Saturday of each month at Hove Library. For more details email:
comedyoferrors@hotmail.co.uk